I0690594

BAD BOYS
ARE GOOD TOO

First Edition

Published by The Nazca Plains Corporation
Las Vegas, Nevada
2009

ISBN: 978-1-935509-21-9

Published by

The Nazca Plains Corporation ®
4640 Paradise Rd, Suite 141
Las Vegas NV 89109-8000

PUBLISHER'S NOTE
Bad Boys Are Good Too is a work of fiction created wholly by
David Solomon's imagination. All characters are fictional and any
resemblance to any persons living or deceased is purely by accident. No
portion of this book reflects any real person or events.

Cover Photo, Vish Studio
Art Director, Blake Stephens

DEDICATION

Some of my inspiration came either from things that have happened to me, or my own fantasies, but most came from guys I've talked to in chat rooms. As such, I only know them by their screen names, and in a few cases, their first names. So - thanks so much to: Bobby, Sean and Mike, Craig K, cottagegrovekiddo, Jaybyrd82, pantysissy, Jump69, wes_19, jjjbucks, Jimmy847, happycamper7, RTB2006, twt_01, xyzscott, and all those in the adult industry who have gone before and taken it on the chin, so that all of us can enjoy our free speech and expression rights.

BAD BOYS
ARE GOOD TOO

First Edition

David Solomon

CONTENTS

BAD BOYS
ARE GOOD TOO

Dave and Sara were having one of their typical vacations – they were hopelessly lost! No one could call it a guy thing and blame Dave. He did ask directions. Many times. Nor could anyone blame Sara. The first time they drove anywhere, both of them were equally inept at reading a map or following directions. They had come to Florida from up north and were only trying to find the beach. It was night, and the city was new to them. They weren't used to the smell of salt in the air, which was everywhere, so heavy that the van's windows were shut and the air conditioning was on. They didn't have a street map, so there was really nothing to follow and they were lost.

They married when they were in their twenties, and after nineteen years of marriage, Sara found out Dave was bisexual. She could have followed the advice of the women's rights groups and divorced him so the groups could chalk up one more. Instead, she did the intelligent thing. She did some research and discovered that such a thing wasn't as uncommon as she thought, and decided to see if she could live with it. The result, so far, was a tremendously spiced up sex life for both of them, and tonight they wanted to do some fucking on the beach. If they could only find the fucking beach!

They were driving through a section of the city that was almost deserted. Not a lot of people around to ask directions from, though that hardly ever helped anyway. A few were walking down the street and a few were hanging out on corners. A few hookers around here and there in their tight miniskirts, long legs, and high heels. After several blocks, the hookers turned into boys hustling their butts on the corners.

"Hey," Dave said. "Let's find us a cute guy to play with! Maybe if we make him shoot a load he'll tell us where the beach is."

Sara gasped. "Honey! Come on! We've never done another guy this way before. We don't know how!"

Dave smiled. "Honey," he said, and reached between Sara's legs and rubbed her pussy, "we've never done anything like everything we've been doing lately. This is just one more. Come on, honey, let's give it a go. Some of these guys are probably bi."

"But how do we know they really know what they're doing? Some of them look really young!" Sara said. Now it seemed there were guys everywhere. Damn cute guys, too.

"We know what we're doing, honey," Dave told her. "And these guys are so hot, I don't care if they know what they're doing or not. It'll be a lot of fun just playing around with them."

Sara pointed across the street. "Now *that* one is beautiful!" she said. "He looks just like a young Omar Shariff!" Dave looked on the other side of the street and just about stopped breathing. He *was* beautiful! Dark hair, not long, not too short, a mustache. He walked to a lamp post, raised one arm up and leaned against it. He was wearing some kind of high school looking letter jacket, open. No shirt. When he put his arm up the jacket fell open to reveal a slightly boyish looking, but downright gorgeous chest.

"Wow!" Dave said. "He looks ready!"

Sara giggled. "His pants are so tight! I wonder how long it takes him to put them on."

"He probably doesn't put 'em on," Dave smiled. "Somebody sprays 'em on him!" As they drove past, "Omar" started to cross the street. Dave looked at him through the rear view mirror. "Shit!" he yelled. "Did you see his butt?"

"Now calm down, honey," Sara put her hand on Dave's thigh. "No one else is around. Let's see if we can try him out."

Dave very calmly pushed the accelerator to the floor and did a doughnut in the middle of the street – squealing tires and all. "Omar" barely noticed until Dave pulled over to the curb across the street from him, rolled the window down and called out, "Hey, guy!"

"Omar" slowly walked across the street, tilting his head to see who was in the car. His crotch strained against his jeans, driving Dave nuts. "Omar" leaned against the window, which let his jacket fall open. Dave could check out his chest and belly. His bulge was really prominent. "Omar" looked like he could be in his 20's, but when their eyes met, Dave could see the youth in them. *'Damn,'* Dave thought. *'That high school jacket is probably brand new.'* "Omar" let his eyes scan the street, then settled on Dave, waiting.

"Hi," Dave said. "What's your name?"

"Joey. Ya'll lookin' for some fun tonight?" he asked in a typical southern drawl.

"Hi, Joey. We are if you are," Dave replied. "What's the going rate here?"

"Depends on what ya want."

Dave flicked his eyes toward Sara and asked, "Are you bi?"

Joey leaned over further and looked Sara up and down. Finally Dave got to see him smile. "Fuck yeah!" Joey said, "Want me to do ya both?"

Dave had to ask. "How old are ya, Joey?"

Joey shook his head. "Old enough – I don't carry no ID when I do this. You gotta trust me. Want me to do ya both?"

"Yeah," Dave said. "And we want to do you. At least I do."

"Fine," Joey shrugged. "Two hundred bucks I'll do ya both."

"That's the going rate?" Dave smiled.

Joey leaned over and looked Sara over again. He winked. "You guys ain't from here are ya? Tell ya what. 150 bucks I'll do ya both. Welcome to fuckin' Florida."

Dave thought, *'He's too young to know how to ask for money. The boys at home would want twice as much, plus a hotel room.'* Dave nodded, "150 bucks. You got it, Joey. Tell ya what. If we all three cum together, I'll throw in the extra 50 bucks."

Joey just shook his head and smiled. "I ain't promisin' that. 'Sides, I only really need 150 more bucks. I don't charge as much as the other guys do. 150 bucks I'll do ya both. You cum when ya want."

In spite of the bargaining, Dave was something of a sucker for young guys who were in situations that made them take risks that guys their age shouldn't be saddled with. "150 bucks won't buy you stuff for very long, Joey," Dave said, thinking about the stories he'd heard of young gays living on the streets because their parents had no guts or brains to deal with their kids being gay, or even have the intelligence to learn something about it – and so, kicked them out of the house.

But Joey just shook his head again. "Look, mister," he told Dave. "I'm only doin' this so I can buy my girl some earrings for her birthday, okay? I only come here when I need extra cash. I got a place to live. So what's it gonna be?"

Dave pulled out his wallet. He took a 100 and a 50 dollar bill out. Then he let two more 100 dollar bills show and looked at Joey. "Tell ya what, Joey. You let us watch ya fuck your girl, and these two friends are yours."

Joey jumped back. He stared at the four bills for a few seconds then shook his head. "She ain't into this shit," he told Dave. "She don't even know I do this. No, man. Just the 150 bucks and you get all of me. Right here, right now." But his eyes were still on the larger bills.

Dave didn't want to hand Joey the money and watch him take off down the street with it, so he reached back and put the bills on the back seat of his van. "Get in, Joey," he said. As Joey walked around the car Dave said to Sara out of the corner of his mouth, "How'd I do?"

"How should I know?" Sara hissed. "At least it worked."

Joey slid into the back seat of the van and pocketed the bills.

"I'm Dave, this is Sara."

"Hi, Joey," Sara smiled.

"Hey," Joey smiled back.

"By the way, Joey," Dave asked. "Where the hell is the damn beach?!"

Joey gave him a strange look, then a smile. He pointed in the only direction Dave and Sara hadn't tried yet. "Two blocks that way. If your windows was open, you'd hear the waves."

"Oh, shit!" Dave groaned.

Joey leaned up and put his arms around both of them. "Welcome to fuckin' Florida!" he laughed.

Fifteen minutes later the three of them were naked on the beach. Joey was on his back with his feet up in the air. Dave was slamming his dick into Joey's ass while Sara smeared her pussy all over Joey's face. Sara leaned forward and started sucking hell out of Joey's dick. Joey tried to moan, but Sara's cunt was really dripping and Joey could only make gurgling noises. Dave had his head thrown back and was panting and sweating with each thrust. Sara rose up and jacked Joey's cock. Dave looked at her, then leaned over and tasted Joey's cock on her tongue. Joey was bucking his hips and meeting each one of Dave's thrusts. *'Shit!'* Dave thought. *'He's young, but he's good!'* He started pounding Joey's tight little hole even harder, and could tell Joey was still wanting more.

Dave met Sara's eyes and glanced down at Joey's dick. Sara got the message. She let her cunt slide over Joey's face a couple more times then turned around. Dave spread his own legs further apart to drop down lower, and pushed Joey's legs apart until they were almost pressed down on the blanket; making Joey resemble a frog. Sara straddled Joey and lowered her pussy down on his cock. Joey's eyes bugged out. "Yeah!" he growled. His face was shiny and wet. Even the front of his hair was soaked with Sara's cunt juice. Joey reached up and played with Sara's tits while Sara used her pussy to jack Joey's cock.

Dave pounded away on Joey's ass; his sweaty chest every now and then slamming up against Sara's back while she bounced up and down Joey's shaft.

"Oh, fuck!" Joey whimpered. "Fuck me!" Dave fucked Joey's butt. Sara rode Joey's cock. Joey fucked Sara's pussy and was going nuts. Then, suddenly, he dug his elbows into the ground and used them to brace himself. He bucked his hips, gritted his teeth, and jack hammered his meat into Sara's cunt.

Sara rose up a little and kept still, allowing Joey to drive his young fuck meat up her pussy. "Oooh yesss, Joey!" she breathed. "Fuck me, Joey! Fuck my pussy, baby!" Each time Joey slammed his dick up Sara's hole he also met Dave's dick as it slid up his ass.

'Holy shit!' Dave thought. *'This guy may be a kid, but he's no boy! He is fucking GREAT!'*

Every muscle on Joey's body was standing taunt as he gave Dave and Sara their money's worth and more. Sara leaned forward until her face was almost in Joey's. Their eyes bored into each other's; each concentrating on the slam bang fucking they were giving and getting. Dave was making animal noises as he drilled Joey's hole, and Joey was hissing through his teeth as he drilled Sara's. Sara tried to cheer Joey on in between the thrusts that were coming fast and furious. "Fuck – me – Joey – fuck – me – baby – my – pussy – is – yours – my – pussy – is – all – yours!"

The orgasm started in Sara's pussy and exploded. Shock waves ran down into her toes and all the way up until they jerked her head back; making it look like she was howling at the moon. She was howling all right, but she didn't give a fuck about the moon. Her tits started jiggling on their own as her body was wracked by wave after wave of some of the most intense pleasure she'd ever had.

Seeing her cum, and knowing he did it, drove Joey over the edge. His concrete fuck stick throbbed and pumped his juice up Sara's cunt, and throbbed and pumped and pumped some more. Joey's own head fell back, his mouth formed an "O" as he panted and huffed and came and came. Joey's juice was filling Sara's cunt while Dave's was filling Joey's butt. Dave just stared straight ahead and concentrated all his energy in his hips. Joey's hole was flexing and milking Dave's cock dry. Joey's cum was running out of Sara's cunt and mixing with Dave's cum oozing out of Joey's ass. Finally, Joey relaxed; his body slumped down on the blanket and Dave's cock fell out of Joey's hole with a sucking sound. Sara raised herself off of Joey's dick and collapsed half on and half off of Joey. She leaned over and slowly started licking the sweat off Joey's face while Dave leaned over and licked the cunt juice and cum off Joey's cock. Then, he lay down on the other side of Joey and joined Sara licking Joey's face.

There was a noise out in the darkness that Joey ignored, but got Dave and Sara's attention. A kind of clicking noise. "What kind of animals are those?" Dave asked.

"Those ain't no animals," Joey said. Then he chuckled and put his arms around Dave and Sara and pulled them in close to him. "I forgot to tell you guys. This is a pretty popular place to come fuck at night. Them's people clapping."

"What?" Dave said, and then laughed. "You mean we just put on a show, Joey?" He looked at Sara, who had her hand over her mouth; her eyes wide.

Joey nodded. "Best fuckin' show they *ever* saw!"

"Oh, shit!" Dave laughed and leaned over and kissed Joey. Soon it was a three-way kiss. They heard car doors closing, engines starting, and then fading away.

Dave figured now was the time. "The offer is still good, Joey," he whispered in Joey's ear.

Joey didn't look at Dave; his head just kind of fell in Dave's direction. "Huh?" he asked.

"Four hundred big ones, Joey, and we watch you fuck your girlfriend. How 'bout it?"

Joey sat up and waved his hand. "I can't!" he said. "Look, guys, this was great. Fuckin' great! But she don't know nothin' 'bout me. We only been goin' for a few months. I only done her a few times. She don't know I do this. And she don't know I like dick. No way I could talk her into it." He started feeling around for his clothes. Sara stayed quiet and let Dave and Joey talk.

"She doesn't have to know, Joey," Dave said softly.

Joey turned to look at Dave. "What the fuck does that mean?"

"How old are ya, Joey?" Dave asked again.

"Eighteen."

"For real?"

"Yeah," Joey said. "I ain't lyin', Dave. I'm a senior in high school. Graduate in a few months. I'm legal, don't worry nuthin' 'bout that."

Dave smiled and nodded. "So, you don't really fuck your girl at her house or yours, do ya? You always go someplace else, right?"

"Well, yeah."

"Look, Joey," Dave said. "You tell us when and where. We'll get there early and hide. You bring your girl and fuck her any way you want. We'll watch, get our rocks off, and let you leave first. She doesn't need to know anything else about you, and she doesn't even need to know we're there."

"Well..." Joey hesitated.

Dave didn't really feel bad about pushing Joey. He could tell from the fuck Joey just threw that there was very little Joey hadn't already done, and that teenagers were always ready for a new experience, a new adventure, so he pressed on. "Tell ya what, Joey. I'll give ya two hundred now, and slip another to ya when it's done. How's that?"

Joey thought about it some and began to smile. He looked at Dave. "You'll hide good? She won't know you're there?"

"She won't know a thing, Joey. And hell, even if she does see us that won't tell her we know each other. She'll just think we're a couple of old farts who escaped from the home."

Joey laughed. "Boy, will she be wrong about that!!"

"So you'll do it?" Dave asked.

Joey smiled and confirmed Dave's instincts about horny teenagers. "Yeah."

Dave grabbed his wallet and gave Joey two hundred dollar bills. Joey looked at them for a few seconds like he'd never seen one before. He shoved them in his pants pocket then grabbed Dave and Sara's hand. "Come on, guys. Let's take a dip and wash off."

The three of them ran into the ocean and washed each other off, laughing and splashing and kissing and hugging. Then Joey said he had to start home. "If my dad wakes up and I'm not there, he'll beat my ass black and blue!" Dave glanced at Sara. Her lips were tight.

"How are you getting home, Joey?" Sara asked. "Do you have a car?"

"Nah, I wish," Joey said. "That's okay. I'll get home."

"Come on Joey," Dave said as he stood up. "Tell us which way and we'll take ya home. Just do me one little favor first?"

"What?"

Dave grinned. "Put your pants on last!"

On the way, Joey gave directions and told them where to be tomorrow. They dropped Joey off as near to his home as Joey felt safe letting them, and then drove away. Sara told Dave he shouldn't have pushed so much to have Joey bring his girlfriend. She said Joey may change his mind and not even show up.

Dave shook his head, "I don't care if he doesn't show, honey," he said. "I just wanted him to have the extra money." Sara leaned over and kissed Dave.

Joey told them they were only about 15 minutes from their hotel, and how to get there. But with their sense of direction it took them an hour to find it. It didn't help much that Sara was leaned over and sucking Dave's cock while he drove, and that kind of took his mind off his driving. He didn't complain, though.

—

Dave and Sara looked like newlyweds walking through the bushes, laughing and groping each other. They weren't sure where they were; they were just following Joey's directions, but had to back track and start over twice. You guessed it: they got lost again!

There was something of a trail that, at times, vanished, and Dave had to consult the list of landmarks Joey told him about. They left the bushes and entered a large clearing they were told to expect. They crossed the clearing into the bushes on the other side. Then they encountered many small clearings; some small enough for only one person to lay down and sun bathe. *'So'* Dave thought, *'this is what's called, "The Party Spot" huh? Cool.'* As instructed, they walked straight through four of these small clearings then came into one that had a small drinking fountain. So far so good. They were glad they came early.

The next clearing was the one they wanted. They picked a spot in another small clearing right next to it that provided a good view of Joey's clearing, and spread out their blanket. They sat down and Sara opened the picnic basket and spread out lunch.

"We're awful early," she told Dave.

"That's okay, honey," Dave said. "Gives us time to eat anyway. Besides, I wouldn't have known what to do if we walked right in on them!"

"We would have kept right on walking, of course!" Sara admonished.

"But we're supposed to watch them," Dave insisted. Sara just rolled her eyes and laughed.

They ate their sandwiches and chips, drank their sodas, and Dave took off his shirt to get some of the sun that Florida was famous for. After a few minutes he heard a noise. "They're here!" he said and rolled over to scan the clearing. A couple came into view; obviously high school students, but it wasn't Joey and his girlfriend. They walked on through the clearing and vanished.

"Fuck!" Dave said. "Anyone could decide to stop here before Joey gets here," he told Sara.

"Well, if someone does, we can at least go back and maybe Joey will see us and know something is wrong," Sara said. "There has to be more than one of these clearings they go to. They'll just head for another one. Then we can follow them."

11

"Yeah, I guess so," Dave smiled. "You're gettin' nice and sneaky, honey!" He reached over and started playing with Sara's tits. "I like that!" Then they heard another noise; this time from the opposite direction. But no one came into view. They realized that what they heard was a girl giggling.

"It's those other kids that walked through here," Sara said. "They must have stopped out of view."

"Yeah!" Dave grinned, "and they're startin' to have some fun. Let's go watch them!"

Sara gave Dave's butt a playful slap, "No!" she said. "We'll wait here for Joey. It's still a little early."

"Come on, honey!" Dave pleaded. "We came down here to forget everything else and have some fun. So let's go take a peek. We can get back here when it's time for Joey to show up."

"We might miss them," said Sara. "Besides..."

"What?" Dave asked. Then he grinned and tickled Sara's pussy. "Why do you want to wait for Joey? Come on now. Fess up!"

"Well..." Sara gave Dave a sheepish, somewhat guilty look and murmured something.

Dave leaned over closer to her and teased her. "What? I didn't hear you..."

Sara gave him a stern look. "I said... Joey's cuter, okay?"

Dave laughed. "I knew it!" he teased. "You liked Joey from the first time you saw him. You're the one who pointed him out to me!"

"Well, so what?" Sara said. "I can think guys are cute too, you know!"

"Sure you can, honey. And you're right. I like Joey too. And his cute lil' butt!" Sara elbowed Dave's ribs.

Then Dave realized something. This was the local Lovers Lane, the Inspiration Point. This was where all the high school kids came to make out and fuck. Every city and town had one. Hell, they may get to see quite a bit of action like what was happening on the other side of the clearing.

"I'll tell you one thing, though," Dave said. "Those other two over there?" The two were making a completely different noise now; a noise that was in rhythm. "They have a great idea!" And he leaned over and kissed Sara.

Joey did show. And he did bring his girlfriend. Her name is Regina – Gina for short, Joey told them. Dave and Sara were already naked and Dave's dick was wet. They almost missed the noise of Joey's arrival, which was just about drowned out by the noise Dave and Sara were making. Sara was riding Dave's dick and had to duck away quickly, and wiggle and squirm to get off it. They both had to dig their faces into the blanket to subdue their laughing.

First thing Joey did was wrap Gina up in a hug and kiss her. A real long, wet, sloppy, WE are gonna FUCK kind of kiss. Gina returned the kiss with the same passion and intensity as Joey. '*I don't blame her,*' thought Dave. '*Or him! She is hot!*' Gina was about as tall as Joey, curvy but slim, very light brown hair, almost blonde. Dave couldn't tell if her dark eye brows were make up, or belying her real hair color, but who cares? She looked great! '*Good job, Joey!*' thought Dave.

Joey and Gina finally broke away and Joey spread out a blanket. Gina kicked off her shoes and sat down. Joey did the same and immediately grabbed Gina again and pulled her down while kissing her. They both lay on the blanket, and while their lips were welded together, their hands were almost a blur sliding over each other's bodies. Dave and Sara lay naked together, elbows dug into the ground with their chins in their hands, and smiles on their faces. For the first time in his life, Dave didn't give one thought to his butt getting sunburned. Suddenly, in one smooth motion Joey pulled Gina's jacket and blouse off and was pulling her skirt down. Dave's eyes widened. He looked at Sara. "Damn!" he whispered. "Was that smooth or what?" He was watching the whole time, but didn't even notice Joey unbuttoning the blouse or unzipping the skirt. But Gina was no amateur either. Joey's shirt was off and his pants unzipped almost as fast. *'Wow!'* thought Dave.

Joey pulled Gina up, sat up with her, and in another swift move her bra was on the ground. *'Nice tits,'* thought Dave. Joey lay Gina back down, leaned over and devoured her tongue again. Dave saw one hand play with a tit, and this time he caught the other hand sliding Gina's panties off. Dave smiled and shook his head. *'Joey's something else,'* he thought. *'Not even out of high school yet, but he can uncover some pussy in record time!'*

Sara leaned over to whisper to Dave, "He's good. He's not even looking around to see if we're here."

"I wouldn't either," Dave whispered and jerked his eyes toward Gina, "if I had that to play with. Besides, what's he got to loose? He's already made some extra money and he's gettin' laid too!"

"Well I guess I wouldn't care either," Sara said. She licked Dave's ear. "But I'm talking about him!" Dave reached over and gave her butt a playful little slap – before he remembered that slaps make noise.

"What was that?" Gina hissed.

"Nuthin' babe," Joey murmured, and went for her lips again.

Gina's hand went to the waistband of Joey's pants. When she pushed them down to uncover his butt, Dave closed his eyes and remembered how much fun it was to fuck that little butt last night. Dave had to roll onto his side and stroke his own cock.

Gina pushed Joey's pants down as far as she could reach. Joey stayed on top of her and scissored his legs until his pants were off. He wasn't wearing any underwear, and now both of them were naked out in the sun. As though she knew there was an audience, Gina's hands went to Joey's ass and pulled the cheeks apart, showing Dave and Sara his little fuck hole. Dave started stroking his dick faster.

Joey slid down and started sucking on Gina's tits. Even though they weren't right next to them, Dave and Sara could see Gina's nipples stand straight up and get sucked into Joey's mouth. Now it was Sara's turn to roll onto her side with one hand playing with her own tits, and the other playing with her cunt. Sara closed her eyes and, again without thinking, she let out a little moan.

Gina again said, "What was that? Somebody's here!'

"It's nuthin, babe," Joey said as he switched tits. "Somebody's always here. You know that."

"It sounded awful close," Gina said. "Maybe we should have gone someplace else, Joey."

"Don't worry about it," Joey murmured between licks. "All the guys know this is my favorite place. They all stay away. Maybe we can hear, but that don't mean any one can see." He went back to Gina's tits and slid a hand down to her pussy. It came away wet. Gina forgot about the noise and relaxed.

Joey rolled off Gina and she eased him onto his back. She got up on her knees and leaned over Joey. She grabbed his cock and stood it up straight. Joey opened his legs a little and put his hands behind his head. Gina leaned down and kissed the head of Joey's dick, then slowly, but in one motion swallowed it whole. Dave couldn't just lay there and watch. Watching two hot young bodies working each other was too much for him. He squirmed around and stuck his own cock in Sara's mouth, and while Sara tried to suck, they both maneuvered themselves so they could both watch.

It was obvious Gina was no virgin either by the way her head bobbed up and down, and got Joey's cock all wet and slippery. Joey was cheering her on with his moaning and repeated, "Yeah's," and, "Yesss's" He started bucking his hips and fucking Gina's mouth without holding her head still. That made Dave suddenly start bucking his own hips hard. But a little too suddenly and a little too hard – Sara gagged. Gina's head snapped up.

"Who's there?" She demanded. Joey rose up on his elbows and tried to calm her down.

"Come on, babe! Don't stop now," he pleaded, but Gina jumped to her feet, oblivious of her nakedness. The bushes that separated all the clearings averaged only about waist high, so anyone trying to be sneaky had to do it laying down. Dave looked away and continued to pump Sara's face, as though he hadn't heard. Gina sat back down quickly and put a finger to her lips at Joey, telling him to be quiet. She leaned over to him. "Somebody's fucking right over there!" She told him and snickered. Joey thought this was the end of it, and he wouldn't get his extra money. He even started to sit up while looking around for his clothes.

"Let's sneak over there and watch them!" Gina said

Joey couldn't believe what he just heard. He just looked at Gina with his eyes bugged out and almost fell back down. "Huh?" was all he could manage.

Gina grabbed his hand and pulled. "Let's *go*!" she whispered, and began crawling on her hands and knees toward the bushes, pulling Joey with her.

'Oh shit!' Joey thought. 'Now *what do I do? What the fuck is* she *doing? This is fucked up! This is all backward. Now I gotta give them the money back.*'

Dave and Sara had been trying to act as though they didn't know anyone was around. Dave got between Sara's legs and started eating her pussy while still keeping an eye on the other two. Sara was trying to roll on her side and suck Dave's dick in a way so she could also watch out for themselves. But they both couldn't look in the same direction at once. Dave tried to move Sara around so he could eat and watch, and Sara tried to bend Dave's dick around so she could suck and watch. They tried to act natural but only ended up looking silly. When Gina first got up on her knees and looked away from them to grab Joey's hand Dave spun around and stuck his dick in Sara's cunt and started humping. Now Sara could bend her head back and watch.

When Joey and Gina started crawling towards the bushes Dave and Sara did what anyone would do who could stay calm in such a situation: they kept right on fucking. In seconds, Joey and Gina were too close for eye contact, so Dave and Sara averted their eyes and pretended to be oblivious.

Gina crawled up to the bushes and ducked down low. She reached out and very slowly parted a branch. Then she turned to a still confused Joey. "There's an older couple in there, and they're fucking!" she whispered excitedly. Joey could only shrug his shoulders. Gina turned back to watch and Joey just looked up at the sky. One would think he was praying. He thought Gina to have been the type of girl who would grab her clothes in panic and run away. Then Joey would not only loose the best pussy around, but he would be out several hundred bucks too! If this didn't work he had no intention of keeping the money.

But instead, Gina grabbed his hand and pulled him closer, a big smile on her face. She put a finger to her lips and jerked another toward the bushes telling Joey to take a look. So Joey parted the branch and smiled a little at Dave humping Sara. Dave's eyes glanced up and saw Joey. Dave looked back down at Sara, then back up to Joey. Dave could only shrug, give Joey a pleading look that meant, "What *else* are we supposed to do? We're fucking *naked*, man!" and keep right on hammering Sara's cunt.

Gina wanted to watch some more, so she reached between Joey's legs, grabbed his swinging cock, used it to pull him backwards and out of the way, and took his place between the branches. Joey saw her hand slide down between her own legs and she started fingering her own pussy.

'Oh, what the fuck!' Joey thought. *'If I ain't never gonna get that cunt no more after this, I might as well say fuck the whole thing and get me a good piece today!'* So, without Gina noticing, he got up on his knees and positioned himself behind her. He grabbed his own dick and with a flex of his hips shoved the head right inside Gina's wet cunt.

That move certainly took Gina by surprise. In fact, she was so shocked that she whooped, and tried to jump up and turn away so she wouldn't be seen. But her knees buckled, her feet slipped in the sandy ground, and, instead of turning away, she fell right between the bushes into Dave and Sara's clearing, and came to rest with her eyes only inches from Dave and Sara's.

Everybody froze. Dave with his dick half in and half out of Sara's pussy, his bugged out eyes locked on Gina's, equally wide. Sara's eyes were just as big and locked on Gina's. Joey groaned. Both Dave and Joey's cocks immediately went soft.

The only thing Dave could think to do was give Gina a guilty, big, Cheshire Cat smile, and say, "Uh...er...um...heh heh...Hi guys!"

—

"*Oh my God!!*" Gina yelled. Dave and Sara's eyes moved as one to Joey, who's eyes were shut tight.

"I'm so glad it's you!" Gina said excitedly. Now three pairs of wide open eyes turned as one toward Gina. She had Joey's full attention now. Gina turned toward Joey. "Look, baby! Look who it is!"

'*What the fuck is going on?*' thought Dave. '*Does she know us?*'

'*What the fuck is going on?*' thought Sara. '*Did Dave fuck her already?*'

'*What the fuck is going on?*' thought Joey. '*Did she already fuck them?*'

"Uh, what are you talking about, babe?" Joey slowly asked Gina.

Gina looked back at Dave and Sara. "I'm just so glad it's you," she repeated. "I thought you were some of the other kids from school, and you'd know it was us, and you'd blab it all over school, and I'd just die!"

Three people had been sitting, kneeling, and laying, all tensed up, and all tensions went out of them at the same time. One could almost feel the air move as all three exhaled their relief.

Dave smiled at Gina. "Well, we won't tell any one at all...uh..." and he looked at Gina expectantly, then at Joey.

Suddenly, Joey woke up, and remembered no one was supposed to know anyone. "I'm Joey!" he almost yelled, too quickly. He pointed to Gina and almost jabbed her back. "This is my girlfriend. Her name is Gina!" Then from behind Gina he winked at Dave and Sara.

As though their voices were wired into each other's somehow, Dave and Sara said together as they pointed to each other.

"I'm Dave."

"I'm Sara."

"She's Sara."

"He's Dave."

"She's my wife."

"He's my husband."

"Yeah, I'm her husband."

"I'm her wife. I mean *his* wife. Oh…"

Then Gina laughed and Joey snickered and the ice was broken. Dave sat up on his knees and Gina looked down.

"Hey, Dave, nice cock!" she said and smiled. Joey just stared at her. He was giving up on being surprised.

Dave smiled at Gina. "Well, thanks, Gina!…um…nice, uh…tits."

Sara sat up and looked at Joey with a conniving look on her face and a sexy little smile. "Hi Joey," she said. "Real nice dick!" Joey just laughed and fell back on his side.

Gina seemed not at all embarrassed about being naked in front of strangers, which surprised them all, but any onlookers would be able to tell that Joey and Dave thoroughly enjoyed it. "Hey Dave," Gina said. "I saw you eating Sara's pussy. It was so hot! I wish you could teach Joey to eat pussy like that. He never has, you know."

Joey almost choked on his own spit. He started coughing and gagging for a minute while Dave and Sara laughed. After all, Joey had a whole face full of some real nice pussy just last night.

"Sure, honey!" Sara teased both the guys. "Teach Joey how to eat pussy! He can practice on me!"

Joey was going just about nuts trying to take it all in. Here was his girlfriend – the proper cheerleader at school who made all the guys wish they were him – talking like a common slut. Saying the stuff that Joey liked to hear!

Gina leaned over and started patting Joey's back. "That's okay, baby. I've been wanting you to eat my pussy ever since we met. Now we've got a couple of experts here! Let's make the most of it!" Joey just stared at her.

"Yeah, Joey," Dave said, looking at Joey with a shit eating grin. "Let's make the most of it, buddy!"

Joey just looked at the three of them, then smiled, shrugged his shoulders and said, "Fuck, yeah! Let's go for it!" Then he grabbed Gina and laid her down on her back. He beckoned to Dave. "Come on, Dave," he said with a wink. "Show me how it's done."

Dave wasted no time. In seconds he was stretched out between Gina's thighs pushing her knees up to her tits. Joey got down close and watched Dave's tongue dart in and out of his girlfriend's snatch and lick that young pussy up and down.

"Oh, my God!" Gina yelled and squirmed. "That feels sooo goood!" She squirmed and wiggled and Dave licked and licked. Joey watched as Dave's tongue fucked his girlfriend. He knew Dave was tasting not only Gina's cunt but his own precum as well and smiled. He looked up at Sara and licked his lips. Sara smiled at Joey and jerked her eyes to Gina. Joey caught the hint and straddled Gina's face, facing her feet. He bent his cock down and shoved it into Gina's mouth. Gina took it and started sucking Joey's dick like she'd never sucked before, and that brought an instant grin to Joey's face. Sara leaned over and put her hand behind Joey's head. Joey leaned over and kissed Sara while he fucked Gina's face.

Sara moved her lips to Joey's ear. "He wants you, too," she whispered. Joey looked at her. "He wants you with him. He wants to share her pussy with you." She guided Joey's head, and pushed him down so his face was right next to Dave's. Then Joey and Dave were both working Gina's cunt.

Now Gina had two hot tongues paying attention to her snatch, and that drove her wild. She started whimpering and sucking hard on Joey's cock. Joey no longer had to hump her face. Gina was bobbing her head back and forth and swallowing Joey's dick over and over again. Joey felt like she was trying to suck it right off and swallow it whole. That made him get right down next to Dave and their tongues starting fighting each other's for a place in Gina's cunt.

Sara lay down and ate Dave's ass while Dave and Joey ate Gina's pussy and sucked each other's tongues and licked each other's faces, and Gina sucked dick. Everyone was squirming so much, that poor little blanket got the worst of it. It was wrinkled up and squished flat. But four people were getting the best of it. Joey couldn't believe his luck. He was finding out his oh-so proper girlfriend was doing the kind of fucking he liked to do. No making love here – not now. Now was just plain ole good time fucking. No worries about performance, no worries about pleasing your partner. No worries, no love, no commitment, just get down, get dirty, and get fucked!

Suddenly, Gina started bucking her hips like she was having some kind of seizure. She yanked Joey's dick out of her mouth and started panting and moaning, her voice getting higher and higher. Dave moved his face out of the way and let Joey lean forward and sink his tongue up Gina's cunt and finish her off. Dave reached around and tweaked Gina's clit while Joey slurped up her juice and Gina went nuts! She reached up and jacked Joey's dick and screamed and came and bucked and came and howled and came some more. Finally, every muscle in her body relaxed.

Joey raised his shiny wet face and grinned at Dave, who winked. Sara got her face out of Dave's butt and laid down right next to Gina, who was sweating and panting.

Dave's eyes bored into Joey's. Dave jerked his eyes to Sara and put his hand up on Joey's shoulder and gave him a slight push. Joey got the signal and scrambled off of Gina. Dave immediately rose up and lay right on top of Gina and kissed her. Gina sucked Dave's tongue right into her mouth. While they kissed Dave slid his hard cock up Gina's sloppy wet pussy and started humping away. Gina's eyes flew open when she realized things weren't done yet. She wrapped her legs around Dave and held him there. Sara grabbed Joey and started to pull him on top of her but Joey didn't need any help. He spun around, got between Sara's legs, and started fucking her like Dave was fucking Gina. Now there were two pairs of legs wrapped around two butts, Joey fucked Sara hard, fast, furious, and grunted like an animal, while Dave sunk his cock into some sweet 18 year old pussy and just fucking wallowed in it, and man I tell you what, but there was some slippery nasty sweaty fuckin' going on in that clearing!

Dave was on top of Joey's girlfriend giving her cunt a pounding, and right next to them, Joey was on top of Dave's wife sinking his dick in her snatch. They were both fucking away on each other's women, looking at each other, and smiling. Dave reached over and put his arm around Joey and Joey put his arm around Dave. The four of them fucked like that under the sun, and sweated and grunted and grinned until all four of them came hard and loud and furious. Dave and Joey didn't notice that they rammed those cunts so hard that all four of them had slowly but surely scooted a few feet from where they started.

Joey slid off of Sara and rolled over onto his back, squirming between the women, his dick not yet starting to go soft. Dave rose up on his knees and his dick fell out of Gina's cunt. All four of them stayed quiet except for their breathing. Two pussies were just trying to close, almost as if they were scared of what may happen next. Two cocks were wet and shiny, twitching a little like they were looking for another target.

Dave glanced over at Joey. Joey had the biggest shit eating grin on his face! He looked at Dave and their eyes met. After a second Joey glanced down at his cock then back up at Dave. Dave caught the look and his face broke out in a huge grin of his own. Dave's shoulders shrugged just slightly – only Joey caught the movement. It was like both of them thought, *"Why the fuck not?"* Then right in front of Gina, Dave leaned over and started licking Joey's cock clean.

Joey glanced over to see Gina's reaction but her eyes were still rolled back in her head. Then he just thought, *'Oh fuck it all!'* He rolled up onto his side and pulled Dave closer to him. Dave's dick was coated with Gina's pussy juice and Joey slowly licked it off, then sucked Dave's dick up into his mouth while he felt his own dick slide into Dave's mouth, and Dave and Joey started a 69 right between their women. Then Joey felt a tongue slide across his fuck hole and realized that Sara had turned around and was eating his ass. That made him suck Dave even harder and he felt Dave's dick get harder and harder in his mouth. He sucked a few drops of left over cum from the head of Dave's dick, and when he stopped for a second to swallow, he could still hear the sound of his lips smacking. Then he realized that it wasn't his lips that were smacking, and wondered what was going on. He opened his eyes just as Dave parted his legs a little.

'Goddamn!' Joey thought as he almost bumped into Gina. *'That little slut!'* he smiled. Gina had rolled over and was eating Dave's ass with the same gusto that Sara was eating Joey's.

Joey stuck Dave's dick back into his mouth and sucked away. He sucked and licked, and sucked Dave's balls and licked his way to Dave's hole where his tongue met Gina's, and the two of them licked and made out right in Dave's butt. Joey could feel that Dave and Sara had the same idea as two tongues started vying for a spot up his own ass. He raised one leg and draped it over one of them to give them more room, and the four of them went at it again.

No one would be able to tell if it was spit or pussy juice or cum or sweat, but all four of them were wet and shiny. Sara and Gina were squirming around trying to eat butt and finger their own cunts. When Sara wanted to lick Joey's hole she would grab his dick, bend it down and stuff it in Dave's mouth to get him out of the way. Then she went crazy on Joey's butt. Gina was having a great time gnawing on Dave's hole. She licked

and sucked it and Dave could even feel her teeth raking across it. He
started bucking his hips trying to get more of Gina's face in his butt.
Anyone in hearing distance would hear the unmistakable noise of fuck.
Dave wondered if they were putting on yet another show for some other
high school kids. *'Who fucking cares?'* Dave thought. *'Joey alone could
teach the teachers some stuff!'* and he went on sucking Joey's cock.

Dave squirmed around and wound up on top of Joey. He turned around
and sat on Joey's chest then fed Joey his dick. Gina straddled Joey's hips
and pushed Dave forward until he was in a push-up position with his
cock still in Joey's mouth. Gina grabbed her boyfriend's dick, stood it
straight up, and then sat her pussy down on it. Sara lay down on her
back and spread her legs. Dave looked like he was doing push-ups, with
each down count sinking his cock into Joey's throat, and his face into his
wife's pussy. Gina rode Joey's cock and leaned over to eat more of Dave's
ass. And the noise of fucking went on and on.

Gina could feel Joey's dick throb and she knew he was about to cum
again. But she slid her cunt off it, grabbed hold of Joey's dick and
squeezed hard, not letting him cum. Then, just like she did with Joey,
she reached between Dave's legs and pulled his dick out of Joey's mouth,
and used it to pull Dave down Joey's body until the two dicks met. She
grabbed one of Joey's legs and pushed the knee to his chest. Joey's other
leg automatically followed. Joey shot Gina a look – he didn't think she
would let him go this far. Gina smiled and looked at Joey.

"Go ahead, baby!" she said. "I know you want it. I know you like to get
fucked too!"

Joey's mouth dropped open yet again. Dave lay on top of Joey, looking at
him and smiling. Sara sat up on her elbows and smiled too.

"Wha–what do you mean?" Joey asked Gina.

"Don't forget, I used to go out with Jack," Gina laughed. "He told me all
about how you would drain his cock dry after baseball practice."

"Ah shit!" Joey slumped down. He'd never even thought that Gina would know such a thing. Or that his best college friend, Jack, would tell. But Gina wasn't done yet.

"He also told me he'd hide here and watch you suck his little brother's dick too!" Gina said. Dave and Sara were looking at Joey and laughing.

"Huh?" was once again all Joey could manage.

"Sure!" Gina said. "I always wondered what was going on at their house. Every time I would surprise Jack and go over there, one of them would always come running out of the other's bedroom. So once I went at night and snuck a peek in Jack's window."

Dave thought he would lay on top of Joey and feel Joey's dick go soft as he tried to take all this in. But instead, it got harder.

"Jerry was naked and sweating, and he was fucking the holy shit out of his big brother's ass! And Jack was yelling for more."

"Oh my God!" Joey moaned. So much for secrecy! Jack's brother, Jerry, was Joey's own age, and in the same high school as him and Gina. He thought he'd kept the fun the three of them were having a secret, but learned he hadn't fooled Gina for even a second.

"Don't worry, baby!" Gina laughed. "I know brothers start out by fucking each other a lot – sisters too. And I like fucking you as much as the other guys do. And I don't want to stop. But..." she looked at Dave, "I want to watch him get fucked. I want to watch him get fucked just like he fucks me!"

That was all the encouragement Dave needed. He looked at Joey, who now had a big smile on his face. *'I knew it!'* Dave thought. *'This guy will go for anything! Anything at all!'* So Dave slid down just a little, and his dick almost fell into Joey's waiting butt. Joey arched his hips and let out a moan as Dave's dick slid home all in one smooth motion. Dave gritted his teeth and moaned as he felt Joey's tight little fuck hole wrap itself around his dick and squeeze. Gina laid down and got her face right up close to watch Dave's cock slide in and out of Joey's ass. Joey saw what his girlfriend was doing and decided to lay back and enjoy it. He clamped his hands behind his knees and pulled his legs way back, opening up his hole for Dave. He worked his hole and squeezed Dave's dick even harder. Gina finger fucked herself and watched Dave fuck her boyfriend. Dave gave it all he had and slammed his dick up Joey's butt so hard, he made Joey's hair shake with each thrust.

None of this was getting past Sara. She knew how much Dave liked to get fucked himself, and had a surprise of her own. At home, she would strap on a big 8 inch dildo and pummel Dave's ass with it. Dave didn't know it, but she'd brought it with her. She pulled it out of her bag now. Gina saw it and her eyes went wide. She'd never seen a real dildo before and crawled over to Sara to check it out while Dave went nuts in Joey's butt. Next thing you know, Sara had shown Gina how to strap it on, and Gina stood up with a big rubber dick hanging between her legs, laughing. She held it up and jacked it – a little clumsy at first, but soon got the hang of it.

Dave saw her, and it was too much for him. He reared back and started shooting a load of cum up Joey's ass. Shot after shot and grunt after grunt, and cum was oozing out of Joey's hole once again. Joey gritted his teeth and cheered Dave on, bucking his hips to meet each thrust. He reached to his butt and grabbed Dave's dick – jacking it as Dave came in his ass. Finally Dave gave one last grunt and slammed his dick up Joey's butt and ground it around as his last drop made it's way into Joey's hole. Then he collapsed on the ground, sweating and panting. Joey still had his legs in the air. That gave Sara an idea.

She reached over and grabbed Joey's ankles. Then she pulled. And pulled. Next thing, Joey's back was straight up and down and he was looking up at his own hole. His dick was pointed straight at his own face. Sara then reached over and grabbed the dildo that was strapped to Gina, and guided it to Joey's hole. Gina caught on and put the head of the dildo right up to Joey's hole. Still loosened up from Dave's fucking, and greased up with cum, Joey's hole just opened up by itself, and Gina slid the dildo in up to the hilt. Once more Joey's eyes went wide and he let out a loud, "YEAH!" as he watched his girlfriend fuck his butt.

Again, a little clumsy at first, Gina stood up and pumped the dildo in and out of Joey's butt. Dave lay down on his stomach next to Sara, and they both watched Gina fuck Joey. Gina knew what it felt like to get fucked, and soon worked into a rhythm and gave Joey the same pleasure he'd given her. Now and again Joey would glance over at Dave, and they gave each other a smile and a wink. Dave liked the idea of him and Joey getting fucked by the same dick – sort of.

Gina was getting another surprise. She thought she was going to give her boyfriend the same pleasure he gave her and nothing more, but she was wrong. The base of the dildo was attached to a square of hard rubber. Padded, but still solid. When it was strapped in place, the square sat right over her clit. While she fucked her boyfriend, the square pulled away, and then pressed back against her clit in rhythm, in effect, massaging it. She started moaning at the sensation, and it made her fuck Joey even harder. In just a couple of minutes, she and Joey both were grunting and yelling. Gina's own tits started jiggling on their own as her orgasm exploded.

It was quite a sight to Dave and Sara, seeing Gina standing up with her feet planted apart, her head thrown back, and screaming as orgasmic shocks wracked her body. Dave saw Joey's toes fan out and knew he was gonna shoot, too. And he did. *Damn* did he ever shoot! He reached up and grabbed his own dick. Dave, Sara, and Gina watched as he opened his mouth and shot his cum right down his own throat. Gina went nuts. Sara applauded. Dave smiled and shook his head. Finally the four of them were all lying on the ground, exhausted, panting, and spent.

Then the same noise was heard. The same clicking noise, and Dave realized they had, in fact, put on another show, and the clicking noise was actually subdued applause from elsewhere in all the bushes around them. Joey ignored it as he did last night, but Dave looked at the women, who had their hands up to their mouths, their eyes widened. Then they all laughed, wrapped their arms around each other and kissed.

—

The next morning, Gina had to work, but Joey met Dave and Sara at a restaurant next to the Party Spot. This time, Dave found the place on the first try. Their bags were packed and in the back of the van. They were flying back up north today. Over breakfast, Dave slid two one hundred dollar bills across the table to Joey.

"There ya go, buddy!" Dave said. "You deserve a lot more."

Joey pushed the money back to Dave. "I don't want no money, guys," he said.

"But Joey!" Sara said. "We promised you, and you did earn it. We want you to have it."

"That's right, Joey," Dave said. "That was the deal, and I wasn't kidding about that, or the fact that you deserve a lot more."

Joey just shook his head and pushed the bills over to Dave. Dave looked like he was going to say something, but Joey slammed his hand down over Dave's.

"Better put it back in your pocket," Joey said with a grin. "Or I'll shove it between Sara's tits right here in front of everybody." Sara laughed.

"I guess it might not matter," Dave laughed. "It would just be one more show, right?" He was thinking about the audience of the past couple of days.

Joey laughed too. "Oh, fuck them," he said. "They ain't nuthin' but a bunch of high school kids like me. They's probably with their girlfriends and boyfriends right now practicin' what they seen us do!"

After they laughed, Joey cleared his throat. "Look guys," he said and took a breath. "I ain't no good at this, but let me tell ya. I made enough money from ya'all. I don't want no more. Yesterday was fun. I mean, I had a great time, and it was just fun! That's how I want to remember it. That's how I want to remember you two. I mean, not that it was business, but that you were fun. Besides," he put his hand back on Dave's and looked at him, "you showed me somethin' I didn't know nuthin' 'bout before." He smiled at Dave. "You showed me I got the best pussy this side of the Mason/Dixon line! And.." he put his other hand over Sara's, "you got the best on the other side." Sara smiled at Joey.

"I made enough money to get Gina her present," Joey continued. "I don't go downtown and hustle my butt 'cause I like it. I go just 'cause it's the only way I can make any money, but I only go when I need to, and I ain't gonna need to for a while now. I just want to remember yesterday as one of the best fucks I'll never forget."

"Well, Joey," Dave said, "for a guy who's no good at this you sure do a hell of a job. How about this? When we get home I'll donate the money to some kind of charity that helps gay folks, how's that?"

"Good 'nuf for me!" Joey smiled.

They walked out to the car and Joey held the door open for Sara.

"Well!" Sara smiled. "Thank you, kind sir."

"Oh, great!" Dave laughed. "Now she's a Southern Belle!"

"And a damn gorgeous one, too!" Joey said and bowed as Sara got in the van.

Joey kissed Sara goodbye from her window then walked around to Dave's side. He looked around to make sure no one was watching, then leaned into the window and gave Dave a kiss.

"By the way, Joey," Dave said.

"Yeah?"

"How do I get to the airport?"

"Oh, no!" Joey groaned, and ended up taking a cab home from the airport.

∎

CROSS MY HEART

Eric burst into his apartment; causing the front door to slam against and bounce off the wall, and practically threw his briefcase across the room. "Fucking, lying, silicone slut!" he yelled to no one in particular while the door slammed closed. Good thing – no one else was there. He tore off his suit coat and slammed it to the floor. "Stupid bitch can't even sign her own name unless someone shows her how!" His tie flew somewhere across the room – shoes sailing somewhere else. "If she'd use her fucking brain even half as much as she uses that stinking pussy she might be worth something!" He poured himself a drink at his bar and gulped it down in one swallow, then poured another... "But I doubt it... *shit*!" he yelled as he yanked his shirt open; buttons bouncing across the hardwood floor. The shirt ended up across the bar while his t-shirt landed on the floor behind the bar. He kicked his shoes and pants off as he poured himself a third drink then stomped across the room and almost threw himself on his sofa, now down to his underwear. He raised a foot and kicked the coffee table away.

Obviously, Eric was a tad miffed. At 29, he was a middle manager in his company, and was up for a promotion to senior management. Today he learned he'd lost the promotion to a co-worker (A co-worker whom one would think he didn't much care for). He gulped down his third straight drink and almost broke the glass slamming it down on the coffee table. He went to his treadmill and started it up at a full run. Soon the sweat was pouring off his body.

"Not one fucking brain cell in that head!" he told himself. "All the bitch did was fuck her way to the top! Fucking cunts always whining about equal rights. If things were equal I should be able to fuck *my* way to the top, too!" He turned off the treadmill and headed into the bathroom. He stripped off his underwear while he turned the shower on full blast and stepped under the spray. He started soaping himself down, and when he started to soap his dick he thought of Trev.

Yeah! That's what he'd do! He'd go see his best fuck buddy, Trev. Trev always made him feel good. Not just for the moment, or just to bend over for him, but to take care of him, calm him down, make him feel good about himself, and send his head up in the clouds.

Trevor was a year younger than Eric. They'd been best friends since elementary school. They grew up together and discovered together that they were gay, popped each other's cherries, and became fuck buddies 'til the end. One would think they would have ended up in an officially committed relationship, but things happened as they usually do. They didn't break up at all, but ended up going to different colleges after high school. Trevor graduated and came back home while Eric stayed in school to earn his masters, so they were apart for several years. When Eric did come home, he and Trevor got jobs in different parts of the city. They lived in a big city and wound up living at opposite ends of it. Going to see each other took a bit of planning, and was at least an overnighter. They stayed best friends, and even though they both met and fucked around with other guys, they remained loyal fuck buddies.

Eric stepped out of the shower, toweled off quickly, stayed naked and went into his bedroom. He dialed Trevor's number and got his voice mail. No surprise there, but this time he decided against leaving a message, and chose to just drive on over to Trevor's apartment with a bottle of wine under his arm, a thong under his jeans, a smile under seductively raised eyebrows, and surprise his buddy. Whether or not Trevor was home wasn't an issue, as both had keys to each other's apartments. Eric figured he'd surprise Trevor by lying in his bed wearing just the thong and his smile.

During the drive through the city, Eric contemplated his situation. The senior partners in his firm were obviously straight as arrows, and it was well known around the executive washroom what went on in their offices with their girlfriends after hours. The office Christmas parties were legendary in hushed circles – especially since wives were never in attendance. Once, a few years ago, someone tried to blow the whistle on the goings on there. That someone now lives in a different city and refuses to talk about it. Everything was very carefully legal, and all the employees since then certainly knew who the bosses were, and knew better than to try to make waves. In many ways a progressive company, Eric thought, but there was a strict division between the staff and senior management.

That was the wall Eric had to penetrate. He was sure the bitch who got promoted was a token. Someone to break the glass ceiling and be put on display. In an effort to prove that the firm practiced equal opportunity, more qualified male applicants were passed over. Eric wasn't the only one passed over, but that cunt was the only female in the running, and another mystery was how she even got in the running in the first place. Maybe it was only a mystery to those who, unlike Eric, didn't work late hours trying to get ahead and heard the noises coming from the top floor offices at night.

An hour later Eric parked his car in the lot of Trevor's complex. He entered the vestibule and buzzed Trevor's apartment. No answer except from Trevor's machine. Eric used his copy of Trevor's key to open the lobby door, went on in and up to the 5th floor. At the door to Trevor's apartment he rang the bell again in case Trevor was there after all. Still no answer, so he let himself in.

He left his shoes and socks by the door. Then he left his jacket on the floor. A few feet more and his shirt hit the floor. Soon there was a trail of clothes on the floor leading to Trevor's bedroom for him to see when he got home. He'd know it was Eric, and that Eric would be waiting for him in the bedroom.

At the door to Trevor's bedroom, however, Eric heard a noise and stopped cold. The door was cracked open, and Eric definitely heard a swishing noise coming from inside. *'Oh, no!'* Eric thought. *'He's got a guy in there! That's why he ignored the buzzer and the bell. He's probably on his back with some guy's cock stuffed up his ass. What the hell do I do now?'* Eric didn't care that Trevor had some other stud in his bed. They both knew that each other fucked around with different guys, and were both cool with it. Hell, sometimes they'd managed a 3 and even a 4 way before, but it was always kind of planned. This time Trevor had no idea Eric was coming over, and Eric didn't feel comfortable at all just walking in on them.

Eric wondered how long it would take him to tip toe back through the apartment, put his clothes back on, and get the hell out of there. He could go back outside, use his cell phone to call Trevor again, and leave a message that he was in the neighborhood and wanted to come over. Trevor would hear the message and either pick up for sure, or call him right back – especially to beg a rain check if he wanted to be alone with the guy. Even so – one more thing was nagging at the back of Eric's head... who was the guy? What did he look like?

Eric decided to sneak a peek into the bedroom. Should be safe. Unless Trevor re-arranged the furniture, all Eric would see would be Trevor's feet up in the air and the guy's butt humping up and down anyway.

Knowing that most people who hear a noise at a door will instinctively look toward the height they would expect to see a face, Eric got down on his hands and knees with his face near the floor. When he peeked around the door, his mouth dropped open and his eyes widened. It was a girl! A *girl!* She had a pair of headphones on, and was dancing around with her back to Eric; her short dress swishing around.

Eric almost threw himself out of the way, spun around, and wound up sitting with his back up against the wall, his knees practically framing his face, and the cock that was getting hard a moment ago hanging limp out the side of the thong. *'Omigod!'* Eric thought. *'It's a girl! He's got a fucking girl in there!'* Then his expression changed to reflect his confusion. *'What'd he do that for?'*

Eric brought his hands up to his face, eyes wide, staring at nothing in particular. *'What the hell is going* on *here?'* he asked himself. *'Is Trev bi? No! Trev's not bi. If he was bi, I'd know and I know he's not bi! So what the fuck is he doing with a girl? Is he experimenting? Nah, he wouldn't go* that *far! I know he didn't go straight.* His eyes widened even further. *Oh no! What if he joined one of those "We Can Change" brainwashing groups, and they told him to go fuck a girl?'*

Finally, it occurred to Eric that he was sitting on the floor next to his best friend's bedroom, who didn't know he was there, and he was almost naked except for a thong that wasn't covering a damn thing anymore, and there was a *girl* in his buddy's bedroom. Eric lunged forward and ended up crawling on his hands and knees towards the front door, snatching up articles of clothing along the way. His only thought at that point was just to get the fuck out of there before he got caught.

He even had his hand on the door knob before it further occurred to him that he would fare much better out in the hallway if he put his clothes back on *before* he left the apartment. So he ducked around the corner into the kitchen and kicked his legs into his pants. He stuffed his socks into his pocket and jammed his feet into his shoes. He stuffed his t-shirt into his jacket pocket, all the while glancing in the direction of the bedroom – trying to think of what he could possibly say if one of them walked out of the bedroom and found him. After a second thought, he decided to hell with the shirt, and just put his jacket on over his bare chest and stuffed his shirt into the other jacket pocket. With one last look towards the bedroom, he tip toed – very quickly – to the door, wrenched it open, almost fell out into the hallway, shut the door behind him, and leaned against the wall gulping in air as if he'd just run a few miles.

"Are you allright, sir?" a voice asked. Eric looked to his side to see a couple of women who had stopped several feet away down the hallway, eying him strangely. They'd obviously seen him explode out of Trevor's door, and he couldn't imagine what they must be thinking.

Eric nodded at them. *"Fine!"* he blurted out, "I'm, uh,... I'm fine. Thanks. I'm fine, really." He could only think to keep nodding at them. They glanced at each other. "No no, I'm fine, really I am....thank you....I'm just in a hurry, that's all," he said, and then thought to start walking down the hallway as though he really was in a hurry. When he passed them, they both instinctively moved against the far wall while keeping their eyes on him. Finally, they both gave him a quick smile and nod, and continued on down the hallway – quickly. Eric kept walking to the elevator and pressed the button. He heard the ladies' keys rattle in their doorway. Then he heard them giggle and rolled his eyes.

The elevator doors slid open. The back wall of the elevator was mirrored and suddenly Eric saw what scared the girls. Good thing no one else was in the elevator. He looked at himself in the mirror. His jacket was open showing his bare chest, while his shirt was hanging half out of one of his jacket pockets with his t-shirt sticking out of the other pocket, and his fly was open. 'Awww *shit!*' he thought. While he was zipping things up and stuffing the rest of other things into his pockets, the elevator doors closed again, and the elevator went down without him, and he had to press the button again.

He looked down the hallway at Trevor's door again. *'Shit!'* he thought. *'What am I so fucking scared about? Trev's my best friend. Hell, we just had a wild fuck last weekend! If anything was going on he'd tell me. So what if he has a girl in there? He'd just introduce us and give me some kind of signal if he wanted to be alone with her.'* He shook his head a bit and wondered, *'But why would he want to do that?'* So Eric walked back down the hallway.

He listened at Trevor's door and heard some dishes rattling in the kitchen. He pushed the button and rang the bell again. "Coming!" he heard Trevor's voice call. *'Good,'* he thought. *'Trev will open the door himself.'* But when the door opened, Trevor wasn't the one standing there – it was the girl. The first thought that flashed through Eric's head was that the girl looked a lot like Trevor's sister since the resemblance was striking, but it didn't occur to him that Trev's sister was several years older than Trevor and didn't look like this the last time Eric saw her. She looked at Eric and shock swept over her face.

"Hi," Eric said quickly. He wondered why she looked upset. "I'm Eric, Trevor's friend. Is he here?" She only stood back while Eric entered. "Hey, Trev!" Eric called into the apartment. "Where are ya, buddy?"

The dejected sounding voice came from behind him. "I'm here, Eric." Eric stopped in mid stride. *'Wait,'* he thought. *'How'd he get behind me?'* He thought maybe Trevor was behind the girl and he just didn't notice him. But when he turned around she was the only one there.

"Whaa... what?" Eric stammered.

She shrugged her shoulders and looked down. Then she sighed deeply and said without looking at Eric, "It's me, Eric."

Eric only stared. His mouth slowly dropped open as he realized he was talking to his best buddy, who he thought he knew inside and out. *She* was *him!* "Omigod!" was all Eric could mutter. "Oh my fucking God!... Trev? Is that really you?"

Now Trevor turned his made-up eyes to Eric. He just shrugged again. "Yeah, Eric. It's really me. I... I didn't know you were coming."

"Yeah," Eric said. "I guess you didn't." Eric didn't look for a chair but just leaned against the wall and slid down it until he was sitting on the floor. He didn't take his eyes off Trevor. "Trev... you're going to a masquerade party... aren't you?"

Trevor looked this way and that, as if he was trying to decide something, then took a deep breath and looked Eric in the eye. "I was going out, yeah."

"But not to a masquerade party," Eric said without making it a question.

"No, not really."

"Then where?"

Another shrug. "A bar."

"A bar?" Eric's eyes widened. "A *bar?* You mean you're going out to a drag bar?"

"Well, yeah," Trevor said. "That's usually where you go when you dress up in drag." He tried to sound confident – challenging even – but his voice still had a little quiver, his eyes desperately pleading. "I didn't *know* you were coming, Eric."

Suddenly Eric's face broke into a smile. He let his head fall back until it touched the wall. "*Wow!*" he hollered, then started snickering.

Trevor shifted from one foot to the other, clearly uncomfortable as hell. "Look, Eric..." he stammered, "you weren't supposed to know... I mean... I should have told you, but..."

"Heyyy... " Eric said as he stood up. He walked up to Trevor, cupped his face in both hands and looked him in the eye. "Boyfriend! How could you keep secrets from your best buddy?"

A smile crept onto Trevor's face but he still only shrugged. His eyes started to mist over. "I...well I....," a tear rolled down his cheek, "I didn't want you to get pissed and never talk to me again!" he cried. "You were my only friend. The only guy I could talk to, ever!" Now the tears were flowing freely. Eric took Trevor's hand and led him into the living room, sat him down on the sofa and sat down next to him, still holding his hand. He reached over and handed Trevor a Kleenex.

"Listen to me, babe," he said. "I'm *not* pissed! At least I'm not pissed that you like to cross dress. I'm a little pissed that you think you can't talk to me and tell me stuff, though." Trevor wiped his eyes and blew his nose. He normally had long blonde hair parted in the middle and combed back, but now it was fluffed out and flipped up, and was falling in his face. Eric reached over and brushed it out of his eyes. "How long?" he asked Trevor.

Trevor sighed again. "Since I was 14," he said simply.

Eric almost laughed again. "You're shitin' me!" he chuckled. "But how did you hide it? We did everything together, Trev! How the hell did you keep something like this from me? When the hell did you find time – shit! We spent all our time together, man!"

They sat and talked for a long time. Trevor told Eric about swiping his sister's clothes and underwear from the laundry and playing in them when he was alone. Then, later, when he was old enough to work, he bought some of his own stuff and hid it in the house. He took it to college with him and hooked up with some other cross dressers. He'd take everything to their houses and get made up and dressed up there, and go out with them as a girl. Sometimes he would spend whole weekends with them, and they all stayed dressed up and lived as women. After college, he came back home, and would still dress up and go out to drag bars. He had one set of friends as a guy, and a whole other set of friends as a girl.

Very few guys regularly hung out in drag bars, and very few queens regularly hung out at regular gay bars, so the two groups' paths rarely crossed. Until tonight, that is.

Since they were both best friends, the talk became more and more comfortable, and soon Trevor was sitting wrapped up in Eric's arms and they were both laughing at some of Trevor's stories about his antics as a girl. He let Eric get a close look at his false eyelashes and told him how he learned to fix his hair. He let Eric feel his "breasts" and told him how he did himself up. Eric had some good laughs and made sure he kept calling Trevor "boyfriend" to keep him relaxed. He ran his hand up and down Trevor's leg, felt his stockings, and commented on his shoes.

"You know something?" Eric asked.

"What?"

"You're actually... pretty."

Trevor smiled and looked at him. "You mean it?" he asked in a tiny voice.

"Yeah... I do," Eric answered. "I do. You really *are* pretty, Trev."

"So you're really not pissed?" Trevor asked hopefully.

"Oh *hell* no!" Eric laughed. "Why should I be pissed, babe? Confused a little, yeah. Shocked, bewildered, dazed and amazed maybe, but no way I'm pissed! Don't worry about that! Hey," he said and leaned in so his mouth was right at Trevor's ear, "does this seem like I'm pissed?" he asked softly and slid his hand up Trevor's thigh and up under his dress. He clamped his hand around Trevor's cock inside his panties and squeezed. Trevor sucked in a breath... and Eric laughed.

"What's so fucking funny?" Trevor asked, mock anger in his voice.

"Oh, sorry," Eric laughed. "Well, number one – I never thought I'd *ever* slide my hand up a dress, any dress, and number two – I never thought I'd slide my hand up a dress... and find a cock up there!"

Trevor was obviously relieved as they both fell against each other laughing. Eric kept his hand up Trevor's dress and Trevor slid his hand between Eric's legs and found a hard bulge to play with. Trevor started to lean into Eric, his mouth opening. Eric quickly brought his other hand up to Trevor, and stopped him. "Just do me one favor, babe?" he asked.

"What's that?" Trevor asked.

"Don't smear lipstick all over me?" Eric snickered, then put his hand on the back of Trevor's head, pulled him close and kissed him.

They kissed and made out for a long time, their hands between each other's legs, their cocks getting harder and harder. Trevor unzipped Eric's pants and reached inside. Eric reached inside Trevor's panties and both cocks were getting jacked. Their lips stayed together while Eric kicked his shoes off and heard Trevor do the same.

Trevor broke away and got on his knees in front of Eric. He grabbed Eric's pants and pulled them down and off. Eric pulled his thong down and his cock flopped up and slapped against his belly. Trevor pulled the thong off and pushed Eric's legs apart. Trevor flicked his hair off his face, leaned over and swallowed Eric's cock and started giving him the best blow job Eric could remember. Eric went nuts watching Trevor sucking his cock, watching Trevor's jewelry sparkle and flash and rattle together – his hair flowing like it never did before as Trevor sucked his cock and kissed his balls and licked his shaft and tongued his slit and sucked it all down over and over again until Eric was moaning and bucking his hips and fucking Trevor's face.

Trevor let Eric's cock pop out of his mouth. He stood up, grabbed Eric's hand, and pulled him up off the sofa. "Let's go in the bedroom," he whispered and led the way. Trevor lay back on the bed while Eric got rid of his jacket and stood naked and hard in front of Trevor. Trevor reached under his skirt and pulled his panties off then spread his legs. "Come on, Eric!" Trevor said in a low, sexy voice. "Take me! Hike my skirt up over my waist and fuck my pussy, baby!"

Eric fell on top of Trevor.

Eric didn't know what got into him. Maybe it was relief over the whole situation. Maybe it was the old idea of doing something taboo and getting away with it. Maybe it was the idea of his old buddy being a new guy. Whatever, he was suddenly damn horny, and he wanted to do what Trevor told him to do. He lay on top of Trevor, clamped a lip lock on him, and ground his cock hard into Trevor's. Trevor spread his legs and Eric kissed Trevor's lips and eyes and nose and neck almost as if he had several mouths.

"Oh *God*, Eric!" Trevor moaned. "Oh yes!! Yes!! Do me baby! Do me good! Do me *hard*! Do me Eric – do me *now*!" And he wrapped his legs around Eric and dug his fingers into Eric's back. Eric couldn't talk. His mouth was full of lips and tongue and nose and ear. All he could do was kiss and slurp and moan.

Then Eric's hands woke up. They undid Trevor's blouse and almost ripped it when he yanked it open. Eric reached down and inside the skirt and grabbed Trevor's cock, jacked him hard a few strokes, then slid down further and fingered his ass. His other hand slid up to Trevor's chest and found... a bra!

Eric slid his hand over the bra, pulled on it, stretched it, and kneaded it. He worked his fingers up inside it and pinched Trevor's nipples. Trevor moaned and squirmed, grabbed Eric's fingers and sucked on them then pushed them back inside his bra. Eric rubbed the bra and slid his fingers up and down the strap and across the front. Suddenly, Eric raised himself up like he was doing a push up and was panting. He looked down at Trevor and in a low, husky and horny voice he said between breaths, "How do you do it?"

"Do what, baby?"

Eric nodded to the bra. "How do you take one of these fuckin' things off?"

Trevor went into a fit of laughing. "You mean that's what's you've been trying to do all this time? I thought you were enjoying it!"

"God *Damn* it, Trevor!" Eric said through a smile. "Tell me!" He rammed a couple fingers up Trevor's ass and wiggled them around. "Tell me, Trev! Tell me!"

Trevor gasped and squirmed under Eric. "Okay baby, Okay! But you have to play with my pussy like that some more first!"

Eric slid his body up until his face was right over Trevor, keeping his fingers up Trevor's ass. "Oh, you little *bitch!*" he growled and shoved his tongue in Trevor's mouth. Trevor showed Eric how hungry he was.

Trevor reached down and jacked Eric's cock while they kissed. Eric took his free hand and pushed down on Trevor's forehead to hold him still, then tongue fucked his mouth and finger fucked his ass. When he finally broke away, Trevor recognized the look in Eric's eyes, and knew he was about to get royally fucked. Almost in a panic; Trevor sat up, and reached over to the night table for some lube. He knew he had to grab it himself unless he wanted Eric to shove his cock in dry. Eric's fingers left Trevor's butt, and while Trevor was sitting up, Eric grabbed his bra and yanked it straight up. The bra came off Trevor like a t-shirt just as Trevor had a handful of lube. He barely laid back and got it smeared over his hole in time as Eric's cock threw itself right up Trevor's butt. Eric fell back on top of Trevor, and with his breath hissing through gritted teeth and his eyes squinted shut, Eric went crazy fucking Trevor's little hole. Trevor wrapped his legs around Eric's hips with his arms around Eric's neck and begged him not to stop. Eric had no intention of stopping, and within a minute the mattress was rocking back and forth as the headboard slammed up against the wall, rattling the pictures, and both of them were moaning, grunting, sweating, and fucking.

Trevor reached down, dug his fingers into Eric's butt cheeks, and used them with his own legs to pull Eric's cock into his ass even harder. Eric fucked away and every now and then raised up a little, opened his eyes to bore into Trevor's, then let his eyes roll back in his head. The only other part of his body moving was his hips as he drilled his buddy's ass with animal grunts escaping his mouth like puffs of smoke. All Trevor had to do was take it and love it. That, he did!

Sweaty bodies are slippery bodies, and Eric used that fact to help him slide his whole body up and down on top of Trevor while his cock twitched and throbbed. Trevor knew he was gonna get it now! He raised his feet up in the air while his hands caressed Eric's head and back. "Come on baby," he coaxed, "give it to me! Give it *all* to me... ooooh yessss! Give me that spunk like you always do!" It had been a long time since Trevor needed to jack his cock while being fucked by Eric, so he used his hands to cheer Eric on; squeezing his pecs, his butt cheeks, mussing his hair, and cupping his face. Eric's grunts became more forceful and higher pitched. He suddenly leaned his head down and bit into Trevor's shoulder while he emptied his jizz into Trevor's waiting ass, and felt Trevor's own cum smearing both their bellies.

Afterglow is nice! Some guys shoot a load, and a minute later they're putting their clothes back on, and that's a mistake. Eric and Trevor learned a long time ago that the period right after a great load of cum is shot is when two guys feel the most relaxed and comfortable with each other, so they just lay together. They didn't kiss or talk, but only wrapped themselves around each other and simply enjoyed the feel of each other while they caught their breath. After a while with the same guy, the need to tell each other how great it was goes away, and the same message is conveyed completely with a simple touch. They slowly ran their hands up and down each other's bodies with a little squeeze here and there now and then, and only after their breathing was back to normal did they open their eyes, smile, and finish off with a nice, long, sensual, "I mean it!" kind of kiss.

Eric got up and ran into the bathroom. He didn't have to tell Trevor that he needed to piss; he just went and did it. Trevor knew anyway. When Eric returned to the bedroom Trevor was sitting on the edge of the bed, and even though nothing seemed to show outwardly, Eric knew his buddy. He sat down beside Trevor and put his arm around him. "What's wrong, babe?" he asked.

Trevor shrugged his shoulders and looked at Eric. "Well, now you know," he said.

"Yeah?" Eric asked.

"You still feel the same? Or now that you're empty you sure you're not gonna change your mind about me?" Trevor looked away.

"You mean change my mind... and disappear from your life forever?" Eric asked with a smile.

"Well, you don't have to be so dramatic – but yeah – that's what I mean. If you're gonna, just do me one last favor and do it quick, okay?"

"Heyyy," Eric said again. "Boyfriend! I don't want to go away. And I don't want you to go away either. I want you to go to the bathroom."

"Huh?"

Eric brushed Trevor's hair from his face. "I want you to go to the bathroom and get cleaned up, fix your make up and get yourself all dolled up while I take a shower and use your cologne."

Trevor was surprised. "Really?" he asked hopefully. "What for?"

"Because..." Eric leaned over and kissed Trevor. "I want to take my girl out!"

Trevor almost flew into the bathroom, a huge grin on his face. Eric jumped in the shower, and, after a couple of minutes, the door opened and Trevor – now completely naked with his hair tied back – stepped in. They still went out – they just got started a little late.

—

The bar was called, "The Queen of Hearts." Eric and Trevor arrived just before midnight. From the outside the bar was an unassuming kind of place. A small sign with words lit up around a picture of the appropriate card from a poker deck announced the name of the establishment, but otherwise no fanfare. They had to park a few blocks away, and while they walked Trevor told Eric something about the place.

"It opened sometime around 1967," he told Eric, "and it's always been a drag bar, but in the early days it couldn't be advertised as one. It wasn't safe – not even after Stonewall happened."

"You mean it got raided all the time and stuff?" Eric asked.

Trevor shook his head. "I don't think it was ever raided, but so many places were, so everyone was careful. That's why the sign is so small and all that. The owner never changed it even after it was safe. She's never advertised anywhere either. Everyone just knows it's here and they keep on coming."

"She? You mean a woman owns a gay bar?" Eric asked.

Trevor giggled. "It's not a gay bar – it's a drag bar, and she's a 'he.' But you know what? I've never seen what she looks like as a man 'cause she's always in drag."

"The same person, you mean? Since 1967?"

"Yeah!" Trevor answered. "Isn't it fabulous? She opened it right after she graduated college. She calls herself 'Kitty.' I bet it's a take off on the word 'pussy,' but it's cute. She must be in her 60's by now, but she's there every night. She's a permanent fixture for sure."

"But, aren't all the queens who come here gay?" Eric asked. "Doesn't that make it a gay bar?"

"Yeah, but we've never called it that," Trevor said and shrugged. "Besides, not *all* the queens are gay, but most of us are."

Trevor told Eric more about the early days of the bar. In the beginning it was almost two separate bars. It had a bar in a large front room, and the clientele was a mixed group of men and queens. To the casual observer it looked like any ordinary bar. However, there was a "back" room the same size as the front, where the queens could mix and the guys could be together without fear of the reprisals going on then.

Even though nothing really happened here, there was a plan. The back room could be closed off by a partition that was painted to look like a solid wall – complete with light fixtures that actually worked: quite an accomplishment for 1967. Even the tables in the front room were covered by layers of tablecloths that reached the floor. Someone could actually hide under them if things got that bad. Kitty didn't mess around when she first opened the bar. The building used to be several other businesses over the years and was constantly redecorated and renovated. Many nooks and crannies were created, and Kitty kept most of them, but found clever ways of closing them off – the better to hide someone if the cops ever came for a raid.

They never came for a raid, but once some off duty cops came in just to have a drink. They didn't even know it was a drag bar. All the regulars knew what to do if the bartender rang her bell behind the bar, and Kitty recognized the incoming customers as cops and assumed the worst. She pressed the buzzer under her table with her foot. She didn't see or hear, but knew the bartender saw the lights flash at the cash register and along the bar. The customers who didn't see the lights heard the bell. The entrance to the bar was a little room, behind which a long hallway with a couple of U turns in it led to the bar. The main reason for that, and the requirement to pay a cover charge, have ID's checked, and hands stamped was to stall for time so who ever needed to could run and hide. That night the "drill" proved that all the safe guards were effective – except that they weren't really needed, as the cops only wanted a drink, but all the queens had to stay hidden in the closed off back room until the cops left. They didn't care – at least they now knew the fake wall and all the hidden cubbies did their jobs.

Harassment of gays, and especially queens, was considered sport back then. There was no talk of hate crime legislation or gay rights. The entire bar was always very dark, lighted only by a single candle on each table and a few extras along the bar. In those days, queens were always afraid of being exposed, and the darkness helped hide true identities.

In the late 1970's things were getting better and Kitty redecorated again. She combined the two rooms into one big room, and added a stage and a dance floor. She installed modern plastic tables, but replaced the long tablecloths when she realized she was never going to stop the queens from sucking cock under the tables. That still wasn't a good thing to let cops see!

"Are you sure it's safe to go in there now, Trev?" Eric laughed.

"Oh, it's nothing like that now!" Trevor laughed. "It's a cool place, you'll see. Lots of queens talking our shit, but I love 'em all and I always have a blast here. One thing, though, baby?" he looked at Eric sheepishly.

"What's that?"

"When I'm in drag I'm not Trev – I'm Trish. Okay?"

Eric looked a little surprised, but then it occurred to him that it would in fact be a little silly to be a girl with a man's name. "Okay…Trish," he smiled, "if were going to do this, let's do it right," and he put his arm around Trish's waist and pulled her in close to him as they entered. Trish leaned her head into Eric.

The first thing Eric saw was a big black queen at a counter, checking ID's, taking cover charges, and probably checking coats in the winter. She wasn't fat, just big, like a football player. Eric wanted to laugh but thought better of it. Her make-up wasn't bad, though, and she did a good job with her hair… or wig… or whatever.

She looked up, recognized Trish, and broke into a big smile. "*There* you are, honey!" she cooed, very femmy and a little fake, but still sincere. "'Bout time you got here. Where you been all night, girl?" Then her eyes fell on Eric and her smile grew even bigger. She made a show of leaning over the counter and eyeing Eric up and down. "Oh! I See!" She smiled. "You've been out…" and turned her head to look right in Trish's eyes, "… shopping?"

"Back off bitch, he's mine!" Trish shot back, causing Eric's eyes to widen as he looked at Trish in surprise.

"Oooo honey! We got some sharp teeth tonight don't we?" the queen asked, then laughed. "Don't worry, girlfriend, I'm on the rag this week, so you still got a good chance," she looked again at Eric and smiled.

Trish rolled her eyes. "Eric, I'm afraid the first bitch you gotta see in this place is Marlene here. Marlene, this is Eric – my *boyfriend!* So just retract those claws honey. Save 'em for someone *you* might have a chance with." Eric was thinking he may have to step in between them but they both only laughed. Marlene held out her hand to Eric – not for him to shake, but for him to kiss, which he did: over dramatizing it as the girls have been doing. He looked to Trish for approval and she gave him a quick wink.

Marlene cooed, "Oooo! Chivalry ain't dead *heyah!*" She looked at Trish. "Good job, honey!" She also still held Eric's hand and Eric didn't know what to do.

Trish made a show of reaching up to separate their hands and told Marlene, "Chivalry might not be dead honey, but *you* will be if you don't dry up that cunt and behave your li'l self!"

"*Ouch!*" Marlene yelled, and looked hurt, clutching her chest. "What did I ever do to you, you little slut? Look, Eric," she turned her attention back to him. "Normally the cover charge is 5 dollars each, but any time I'm here, you can – pardon the pun -" and she winked at him, "slide right on in!" Then she jerked her thumb in Trish's direction. "But it'll cost this bitch double to get in here now!" Eric and Trish both just laughed. Eric gave Marlene a 10 dollar bill, which she dramatically stuffed into her bra.

Trish told Eric, "Her tits get bigger as the night goes on."

"Oh, you hush up, girl!" Marlene snapped with a hard look at Trish, "or I'll tell Eric some secrets about you!" She stamped their hands as the two girls giggled and sent them on their way. "Have a good time, kids!" she waved to them.

Eric put his arm around Trish as they walked into the bar and she leaned against him. "What the hell was all *that* about?" Eric asked. "I thought I was gonna see some blood!"

Trish laughed. "Who? Marlene? No way! I love her to death – she's the sweetest girl here. That's just how we have fun."

"Fun?" Eric laughed. "That's how you have fun? Man! I'd hate to see what you two do when you're pissed!"

"Well just let one of these cunts try to get to you and you'll see me get pissed!" Trish warned.

"Mmmm," Eric moaned and smiled. "Is my girlfriend getting possessive… I like it!" and he held her tighter.

As they made their way through the bar, Eric saw right away how popular Trish was. Seems like she knew everyone. Queens came up to her and they clasped hands and hugged and kissed cheeks (without actually touching), and they all complimented Eric and held out their hands for him to kiss; which he did gallantly, and seemed to be getting into it. Of course, the compliments didn't do his ego any harm, and helped get him in the mood. He was a little nervous, though, at all the attention and the fact that he felt a little like an outsider in this bar. There seemed to be some signals being passed, and for once he didn't know what any of them meant. Soon his smile appeared to be planted on his face, and while he was kind of enjoying things, he was glad to finally get to a table and sit down in the near dark.

A waiter approached their table, who, this time, wasn't a queen. He wore a bow tie around his neck but was otherwise topless, and wearing super short shorts which showed off his bulge and his butt. He said hello to Trish, but kept his eyes and smile on Eric as he did so. Trish didn't seem to mind and gave their drink order. Eric knew the waiter was swinging his butt just for him as he walked away.

"He's dreamy, isn't he?" Trish leaned in close and asked.

"Sure is!" said Eric. "Maybe if I decide I don't like queens I might try to get him in... " Trish jammed an elbow in Eric's ribs.

"You better not!" she laughed. "I have no intention of being dumped right in the middle of the bar!" Then she winked at Eric. "Besides, I have a reputation to protect."

"Yeah?" Eric smiled. "A reputation as what? Easy?" They both laughed and their drinks came. Trish quickly dismissed the waiter, but they blew each other a kiss as he walked away.

"His name's Tony," she told Eric. "He's tough to figure out. He never tries to pick any of us up, and we all thought he just didn't like queens. But one night a straight guy came in here who didn't know this was a drag bar. He was already drunk, and when he found out we were all queens he tried to start some trouble. We couldn't believe it but Tony did some kind of karate-like move on him and shut him right up. Grabbed him by his throat and made him apologize to all of us. *Then* he punched him right out, picked him up and literally threw him out the door!"

"No kidding!" Eric said. "Maybe I'd better behave myself in here!"

"Listen," Trish whispered in his ear. "If you ever do get to him you'll have to tell all of us how he is! We're dying to find out if that package of his is real!"

While they talked and drank, Trish pointed out several queens and told Eric about them. They were sitting at a table in the back. One side of the table had a couple of chairs, and the other side was a booth that ran all along the back wall connecting several other tables: some empty, some with other couples sitting at them. Eric and Trish sat in the booth. Other queens who knew Trish stopped by and chatted and laughed and giggled. They all acted like they were trying to hit on Eric, and Trish warned them off with a few choice words that made Eric wince. But then everyone laughed and more drinks came.

"So are you fucking all these guys – uh – girls?" Eric asked.

"Oh, no!" Trish said, shaking her head. "Queens don't have sex with each other. We all wait for hot, horny hunks... like you!" Eric leaned over and kissed her.

"I'll be back in a minute, babe," Trish told Eric. "I need to check my make-up and take a piss." Eric stifled the urge to ask her which bathroom she used. Turns out it would have been a foolish question anyway. Eric watched her slink across the room and saw that both bathrooms were labeled, "Women."

He saw Marlene wave to him as she sashayed her way back to his table. She sat down across from him. "So – having fun?" she asked him.

"Well, yeah," Eric said, "but I do feel a little like a virgin, ya know?"

Marlene put her hand over Eric's. "Look, Eric," she said, "this whole place is nothing more than one big stage, and everyone in here is only playing a part just like Shakespeare said. We're all just having fun, no more, no less. Don't worry, no one means anything they say, and they'll do even less." She looked at Eric closer, "You've never been to a place like this before, right?"

Eric told her about growing up together with Trish and what had happened earlier tonight, leaving out the juicy parts, of course. Marlene asked some questions but wasn't pushy. Eric asked some questions about the bar, and Marlene explained that where they were sitting used to be the secret back room where the queens of the early days could gather and just have fun acting like girls. Eric asked about the owner, Kitty.

"Oh, Kitty still shows up almost every night, but she doesn't stay as long as she used to," Marlene explained. "She's still as feisty and spicy as she always was, but she had a cancer scare a long time ago, and almost had a heart attack recently, so she's been slowing down. She's already been in tonight and gone home."

"But," Eric asked, "how does she keep up with running this place without being here?"

Well, Eric," Marlene said, and looked around to make sure no one was near. Then she leaned closer to him. "No one knows this, but 10 years ago me and a partner bought this place from Kitty. She doesn't run it any more. She's retired. But she's become such an icon here over the years we were afraid that if word got out it would hurt business. So she comes in for us every night, has a good time as long as she can stand it, and everyone thinks things are just fine. I know it's like being dishonest, but I think of it as a smart business move."

"Sounds good to me!" Eric said. "Hell, if it works, it works. So you're really the new Kitty around here, huh? You and your partner?"

"Oh yes, and it's a good thing I'm not into an ego trip about it, too!" Marlene laughed. "I run this place by myself just like Kitty did. My partner is another business man who runs another company." She smiled and leaned closer to Eric. "You'd be real surprised who some of my friends are!" Then she looked around the bar. "Listen Eric, if these girls in here get to be too much, just give me a signal and I'll do something. Quiet – but I know how to handle them. But I'm sure that once you get to know them you'll like them just fine."

Eric looked at her with the corners of his mouth starting to smile. "Wait a minute," he said and pointed a finger at Marlene, "you're not talking like you were earlier."

Marlene laughed. "No, I'm not. For the moment, Eric, it's not Marlene talking to you. I'm Marlon now."

Eric shook his head and rolled his eyes. "Damn!" he said. "How the hell am I supposed to know who's who, and when they're who?" he laughed.

Marlon just smiled. "I told you," he said, "we're all just actors here, and it's all just that, an act. Everyone here – they're all really sweet guys, but even in the "New Millennium" this is still one of the very few places we can come and be who we see as ourselves."

Eric nodded his head. "Okay," he said. "I can sure understand that. I got a little bit of experience trying to get to places that are unreachable to me." And he wound up telling Marlon about where he worked, losing his promotion, and why. Turns out Marlon was a great listener. He asked questions and offered some advice. Then they saw Trish heading back from the bathroom, being stopped by a few tables, with everyone glancing at Eric, and Eric overheard some more of their patter.

"Hey Trish!" someone yelled. "How many times I gotta tell ya to change your tampon *before* you come here?"

"Watch it, bitch!" Trish yelled back amid laughter. "Or I'll pull it out of my cunt and shove it up yours!" Eric shook his head, rolled his eyes, and averted his gaze.

Marlon patted his hand. "Thanks," he said simply. "I hope you have a good time tonight, Eric. We all think a lot of Trish, and we're all just really glad she has someone. And I'm especially glad it's you," he said as he stood up, and suddenly he was Marlene again. "You just let Marlene know, honey, and I'll get aaaaalllllll these wolverines off ya!" she said loud enough for almost everyone to hear. She sashayed her way back through the bar and Eric stared at her with a smile on his face. Trish reached the table and sat down.

"What was that dyke trying to do – pick you up?" she asked Eric in mock anger. Eric just wrapped his arms around Trish and kissed her. "Wow!" Trish said. "I'll have to ask her to try it again!"

They talked and drank and kissed and danced and drank and kissed some more. Queens that came in with boyfriends sat at tables near them, some Trish knew and some she didn't. Some sat close and they introduced themselves and chatted. Some were making out and some were dancing. All were feeling a good buzz by now.

After a particularly fast dance, Eric and Trish collapsed in their booth and ordered fresh drinks. They sat and watched the others and kissed some more. Eric had his hand on Trish's leg, and suddenly Trish reached down and grabbed Eric's cock through his pants.

"Damn, babe!" Eric said. "You wanting to go home?" he asked slyly.

"Home?" she asked. "I can't wait *that* long, honey!"

"Huh?" Eric asked, then gasped, as Trish grabbed his zipper and pulled it down.

"Hey!" he hissed. "What the hell you doing?"

"Don't worry, babe," Trish growled in his ear as she reached in Eric's pants and grabbed his cock through his shorts, "no one is watching – hell, no one can see even if they were watching. It's too dark back here." She pulled his cock out and started stroking it.

Eric's eyes bugged out. "Damnit!" he said. "I can see just fine!" but he didn't make a move to stop her. His cock started waking up and soon stood straight up and proud. Trish leaned over and kissed him, long and slow and deep. When they broke away Eric let his buzzing head fall back, and Trish's head started to move down. Just as Eric said, "Whaaaa... ?" Trish opened her mouth and swallowed Eric's cock.

Eric didn't know what he should do, but he knew what he wanted to do. He glanced around quickly and saw that no one seemed to be watching, so he put his hand on Trish's head to guide her up and down his shaft. He tried not to moan, but it was tough since Trish was such a great cocksucker. He let his hand slide down inside the waistband of her skirt, and played with her butt while she sucked on his cock.

Once Trish got a mouthful of a nice hard dick, she didn't stop. Eric knew that from experience, and soon he felt the crotch of his pants getting wet from her spit, and she just kept right on sucking. She was completely oblivious to anything going on around her. But Eric glanced to his right and saw a guy and his queen openly staring at them with huge smiles on their faces. *'Oh, shit!'* Eric thought, and laughed when he saw the guy quickly give him a thumbs up.

"Trish!" Eric hissed. "Someone is watching us!"

"Ummm Hmmmmm," was all Trish could muster as her lips never left Eric's cock. Obviously, she didn't care. Eric looked around and it seemed like no one else in the place had any idea of what was going on, and when he looked back to his right he saw the guy there getting his own cock sucked. They were close enough that they reached out and shook hands while their queens sucked away. A hard cock reacts to stimuli, and whether Eric knew it or not he'd used one hand to hold Trish's head still while his hips started up by themselves and bucked and his cock fucked Trish's mouth.

Eric saw the other guy's hand waving and looked over at him. The guy pointed to the other side of Eric, and, when Eric turned his head, he saw another guy at the next table, but at first glance, the guy looked like he was alone. Then Eric looked down and saw a pair of heels (with feet in them) sticking out from under the table cloth.

So, now there were three.

The topless waiter walked by with a tray of drinks and almost spilled them doing a double take. Eric thought they'd had it for sure. He tried to quietly tell Trish they should stop, or at least go into the bathroom, but Trish was ignoring him and just sucking and jacking his cock. Finally, he got her attention when he slid his hand inside the back of her skirt and jammed a finger up her hole.

"Oooooo baby!" Trish said after she let Eric's cock fall out of her mouth. She looked up at him and smiled and wiggled her butt.

"Damnit babe! The fucking waiter just saw us!" Eric said in her ear. "We gotta do something!"

"We *are* doing something, honey!" Trish laughed. "Don't tell me you don't feel anything."

"You know what I mean!" Eric said as he pulled her up. She then noticed the action at the next table. "There...you see?" Eric said. "We're gonna get everyone in trouble!"

Trish smiled at the couple at the next table. "Oh, hi Angel!" she hollered to the queen with a mouth full of cock. "Cute trick, honey!"

"Oh, man!" Eric sighed, and let his head fall back to the wall. Obviously he wasn't getting anywhere *this* way.

Trish put her arms around Eric's neck and let him taste his own dick on her tongue. They broke away and Trish leaned over to Eric's ear. "Why do you think it's so dark back here? Neither one of us are virgins, honey, and neither is this place."

"You mean this stuff goes on here all the time?" Eric asked.

"Not every night, but it's been known to happen," Trish cooed in his ear. "Been a long time, though, and seems like now's as good a time as any."

Eric looked to either side of him and saw that those couples weren't slowing down at all. Then he figured, *'What the fuck? The worst that will happen is that we'll get thrown out, and I'm used to that.'* So he grabbed his cock with one hand, Trish's head with the other, pushed her down, and fed her his cock again and shoved it all the way down her throat. "Well, go on then," he told her. "Suck it babe! Suck it good and show all these bitches how it's done!" And that she did. Her head bobbed up and down. A couple times she bobbed up too far and smacked the table – which made the candle flicker – which only drew more attention to them.

"Go *Trish!*" he heard a yell, and saw the waiter walk by again with a big smile on his face. He looked at Eric, winked, and licked his lips. Then Eric heard it start. Only a whisper at first, but he definitely heard some more "Go Trish's," from somewhere. Tough to see in the darkness of the back of the bar, but they certainly had an audience and were being cheered on. Trish obliged by sucking harder, faster, and more dramatically, driving Eric nuts. He'd done some stuff before – playing with guy's cocks under tables in other bars and such, but this was the first time he found himself actually putting on a show on purpose! Maybe it was the whole situation, or the drinks, or both, but it was turning him on, and before he thought about what he was doing he yanked Trish's skirt up over her back so everyone could watch him play with her butt.

"Yeah!" he heard in the darkness. "Do it, guy!" came from somewhere else. Eric looked to his right to see that now the guy had his pants down to his ankles. His queen was going crazy on that hard cock. To his left, he saw the other queen pulling her panties down. In spite of the cheers and other noises, he could still hear the definite sound of a cock popping out of a mouth now and then. Those noises made Eric yank Trish's panties down and she automatically stepped out of them.

Trish suddenly rose up and kissed Eric quickly. Then, before he could say anything, she stood up and straddled his lap with her butt right in his face. "Oh, shit, Trish!" was all Eric got out of his mouth before Trish backed up and Eric found his face buried deep in those cheeks.

He wanted to laugh at the whole idea of the show they were putting on, but instead reached up and spread Trish's cheeks out wide! His tongue flicked out and Trish gasped.

"Oh, my God!" she hollered. "Yes, Eric! Yes baby! Eat my pussy, Eric. Tongue fuck my little hole baby!" Eric did as he was told. If there was enough light everyone would have seen how wet his face got with his own spit as he forgot about everything else except Trish's little fuck hole and how good it tasted. He ignored the cheers and Trish's moans and pleads not to stop, and held those cheeks apart, spread that hole, and licked her inside and out. He ate, licked, kissed, sucked. When he finally jammed a finger up that butt and made Trish gasp again, he glanced to his right and gave the other guy a smile and wink. He looked to his left and saw that the other couple were matching him move for move. He heard another gasp that wasn't Trish. He looked in front of them and growled a quick "Yeah!" as he saw yet another couple in a great looking 69 on the floor between them and the next booth.

And now there were four.

Eric was getting into it. Maybe it was the drink, or just the situation, but he didn't care about anything else now except what he was doing. He shoved a couple fingers up Trish's hole with one hand, and slid his other hand between her legs and pulled her cock back. He heard somebody say, "Yeahhhh," right before he took his girlfriends cock in his mouth and made her gasp yet again! Eric knew just how to suck Trish's cock to get her going good, and it sure worked this time. Eric finger fucked her pussy and sucked her cock 'til she was letting out nothing but one long moan. He heard voices around him – cheering him and the others on, and suddenly he couldn't stand it any more.

Eric jumped up, reached around and wrapped Trish up in a bear hug. He yanked her up so she was standing straight up and she whooped. "So you wanna put on a fuck show, *bitch!?*" he growled and ripped her blouse open. He still didn't know how to take a bra off properly, but right now he was too hot to worry about it, so he just grabbed it and ripped it right off, and everyone saw him grab Trish's tits and pinch the nipples and her mouth dropped wide open.

"Oh, *fuck* yes, Eric!" she moaned. "Oh, shit, baby! Oh, man!"

"Well," Eric was still growling through clenched teeth, "you're gonna get that little pussy *fucked* now!" and he pushed her over the table. He heard the voices chanting as he dropped his pants. As he kicked them off he realized the voices were chanting in rhythm. Not much more above a whisper, but they were saying, "Fuck 'er! Fuck 'er! Fuck 'er," and Eric followed instructions.

Eric let who ever was watching see him spit into his hand and rub it all over his dick. Then he spit some more and smeared it all over Trish's ass. Trish reached out and grabbed the edge of the table just as Eric slid his cock right up her hole all the way, and she threw her head back and just let out a long, "Aaaaaahhhhhh!" Then Eric started fucking and the people cheered. He let them see him slide his dick in and out slow at first, let them see his eyes roll back in his head, and then picked up the pace. He glanced to his left and the queen there was riding her man's cock, and the guy was smiling at Eric.

Eric smiled back and humped away. Trish had completely forgotten about where they were and laid her head down on the table, closed her eyes, and just enjoyed it. She didn't see the couple on the floor get into a butt licking 69, but Eric did, and that made him fuck harder. She didn't see the guy to their right push his queen down to the floor, climb on top of her and start fucking, but Eric did, and that made him fuck faster. All

Trish knew was that she was getting fucked like she hadn't been fucked since she couldn't remember.

Someone reached out and pulled Eric's shirt off, and now he was naked and fucking away. If the light was good enough, he would have looked sexy as hell with the sheen of sweat on his body. Eric saw the waiter, Tony, heading his way. Tony was walking funny, with big steps, raising his feet up high, then Eric realized he was stepping over bodies on the floor. Bodies that were in various stages of a good fuck, and Eric saw that now there were a lot more than four.

Tony walked up to Eric, grasping a water bottle. Laughing, he squirted some water on Eric's face and in his mouth. The water ran down Eric's chest, and Tony leaned over and quickly licked it off Eric's nipple. He turned away to leave but Eric reached out, grabbed the waistband of his shorts and pulled him back. There was a collective gasp as Eric spun Tony around and pulled their faces together and kissed. Eric's cock had a mind of its own (now where have we heard *that* before?), and, while he kept right on fucking Trish, he reached down and unzipped Tony's shorts. They fell and disappeared in the darkness of the floor with everyone else's clothes, and now Tony was wearing nothing but his little bowtie. He climbed up on the table, straddled Trish's body and those closest to them saw that yes; his package *was* real! His cock was long, slender, and hard. Tony grabbed it and Eric opened his mouth. Tony's little bubble butt flexed as he fucked Eric's mouth. Eric sucked cock and fucked butt and joined the growing chorus of moans in the semi darkness.

Outside the bar, people were walking by and didn't even notice. Most of them didn't even know it was a drag bar in the first place. Even if they knew, they didn't notice the "Closed for Repairs" sign that was slipped in the window right before the outside lights were turned off.

The cheers and chants slowly but surely turned into moans and grunts. The couples on either side of them, and the couple on the floor that Eric could see, were fucking like crazy. Noises came from all over and Eric knew what they meant. He moaned himself as his mouth got fucked with Tony's cock. He drilled Trish's ass and reached around Tony to finger fuck his. Tony reached back, grabbed a couple of Eric's fingers, and shoved them up his ass himself. Now Eric was fucking one butt with his cock, another with his fingers, and taking a nice cock down his throat. Now he, too, was oblivious to what was going on around him. There was so much fucking going on in that bar – the only reason anyone went into the bathroom was to piss!

Eric knew he was going to loose it. He didn't want to, but things were just too damn hot. He knew he was going to fill Trish's ass with one of the biggest loads of cum he'd put out in a long time. His own moans started getting higher pitched and Tony picked up the cue. He grabbed Eric's head to hold it still so he could ram that hot throat. Eric moaned and whined and fucked Trish like a damn jackhammer. Trish knew what was coming and her own yells matched Eric's as she heard him let out one long muffled yell around Tony's cock, and pump his spunk up her ass. She opened her eyes and looked straight ahead as her own cock started shooting across the table. She heard another moan above her and that's when she realized that Tony was even there. Trish twisted her head around and looked up just in time to see Tony's little butt flex again as he shot his load into Eric's throat. Eric tried, but he couldn't keep up, and some of Tony's cum dripped off Eric's chin to splat on Trish's ass. She smiled, reached back, and rubbed it in.

That first orgasm, with it's grunts and yells, started a chain reaction, and within seconds they heard the same noises coming from all over. The air quickly filled with the smell of fresh cum. Tony pulled his cock out of Eric's mouth, climbed down off the table, and collapsed in the booth. Eric pulled his cock out of Trish's cunt and fell backwards in the booth next to Tony. Trish stayed splayed out across the table with a huge smile on her face. The couples on either side of them had shot their loads, too, and were just now falling apart. Soon, the only noises left in the bar were the sounds of people catching their breath, and the occasional smacking as everyone gave everyone else a "Thanks for the Fuck" kiss.

It took an hour to leave the bar. First, everyone went into the bathrooms to rinse the sweat, spit, and cum off their faces. Then it took a while to sort out all the clothes that were scattered all over the floor. No one knew where Marlene had been during the whole thing, but now her presence was well known as she scurried through the bar like she was in a panic, telling everyone to hurry up and get dressed and get the hell out of there before the cops noticed the place still had customers in it after it was supposed to be closed. Eric and Trish went naked into the bathroom where they ran right into Marlene; who was standing with her hands on her hips, and a mock angry look on her face.

"Now, Eric!!" she shook a finger at him, "I know I told you to have a good time, but *damn*, man!"

Eric looked at Trish, then back at Marlene, and they all broke up laughing. Eric walked up to Marlene and wrapped her up in a bear hug. "Thanks, Marlene!" he said in her ear. "We'll behave ourselves now."

"Well, you damn well better!" she snickered, and, while looking hard at Trish, she made a show of patting Eric's butt with one hand and squeezing his sticky cock with the other. "Mmm – like I said, honey," she told Trish, "nice job!" and laughed as Eric wiggled his butt in her hand.

Trish smacked Marlene's butt as she ran out the door, then went to the sink where she and Eric washed each other off.

—

A few weeks later, Eric made a frantic phone call to Trevor with an unusual request. He wanted to take Trish out again; this time not to a drag bar, but to a party at his company.

"Excuse me?" Trevor said. "You want me to do what, where? You mean right in the lion's den?" Eric had told Trevor many times of the screwing that went on at night on the top floor.

"I can't help it, Trev!" Eric told him. Then he took a deep breath. "I *got* it man! I fucking *got* it!"

"Got what?" Trevor asked. "Herpes?

"No, damnit!" Eric laughed. "The promotion dude! I got it!"

"No shit? Fantastic baby!!" Trevor yelled into the phone. "But how the hell did it happen? I thought they gave it to that cunt."

Eric told Trevor about being called to the CEO's office on the top floor, and how he was afraid of being fired. The CEO told Eric that the woman they gave the promotion to was screwing up everything she touched, and *she* was fired. He gave Eric a long speech about how the company had screwed up when they insisted the position be filled by either a woman, or someone from a minority group. It was time, he told Eric, that he did his job, and think about what is best for the company and it's customers, and, after reviewing the other applicants, they decided that Eric was far and away the best qualified.

"Actually, Eric," his new boss told him, "a good friend of mine – one of your customers – is familiar with your work, and it was she who brought you to my attention. Hell," he chuckled, "she was up here the other night and saw your file on my desk, and practically shoved it down my throat! I hardly even considered anyone else." Eric dealt with customers all day, every day, and had no clue who he was talking about but didn't care. The promotion was enough.

Then his boss had put his arm around Eric. "Eric," he said, "you know the parties we have here are no secret. This is where we bring our mistresses and you know that too. My mistress was the one who told me about you."

"Yes, sir," Eric replied.

"Even so," his boss went on, "we don't expect any news broadcasts. If you have a problem with all that, tell me now, and you can still keep the promotion or even return to your old job – no hard feelings at all – but what we do here in the evenings will *not* stop. Do I make myself clear?"

"Yes, sir!" Eric smiled. "You do whatever you want to do, sir. I'm only going to work hard to make sure you're not disappointed that you chose me."

It was a political answer and they both knew it, but Eric knew that's the way the game was played. His new boss was satisfied. "Tell you what, Eric," he said. "Let's all get together tomorrow night, right here. You can meet everyone, and then you'll know who we get together with so there won't be any, er, embarrassing moments through the day. Oh – and make sure you bring your girlfriend, too!"

That stopped Eric. He wasn't out at work – not when he worked for well known ultra conservatives. Especially these guys, who, like typical ultraconservatives, had skeletons in their own closets – or on the top floor of this building at night anyway.

He didn't want to tell his boss that, while he wasn't hurting for sex, he didn't have a girlfriend. At the same time, he didn't want to do anything to make waves right off the bat, and that was what prompted his somewhat frantic phone call to Trevor.

"It won't be a big deal, Trev," said Eric. "Just a get acquainted kind of thing. All you'll need to do is shake some hands and say hello to some people, have a couple drinks and all, then we can go out somewhere else."

He heard Trevor laugh over the phone. "Let's see if I got this right," Trevor said. "You want me to dress up as Trish, go to a party with you as your date – in the middle of a bunch of stuffy old men who are straight as arrows, and pass myself off as a woman all night? Are you kidding me, baby?" Then Trevor's voice lowered and sounded seductive. "That's when we do our best work, honey!"

Eric opened his door and there stood Trish. She was wearing a blue evening gown with low heels. Minimal makeup and not a lot of jewelry. She was toned down from the evening at the bar. Eric's eyes popped out. "Wow!" was all he could say. He pulled her into the room and kissed her, then gave her a corsage. As he put his shoes and jacket on, Trish went into the bathroom to check herself.

Eric heard her call from the bathroom, "Hey baby?"

"Yeah?"

"Care to tell me what this is all about?" she asked accusingly as she came from the bathroom with a smile on her face – and twirling a small bow tie in her hand.

Eric just smiled. "Can't you tell?" he asked and winked at her.

"Oh, my God!" Trish laughed. "You've been fucking Tony, haven't you, you sneaky little stud?" Eric just smiled and licked his lips seductively. "Well honey – you have to tell me all about it, and don't you *dare* leave even one detail out!" and she hooked her arm into his as they headed out to the car.

At Eric's company building at that hour the only person at the main reception desk was a security guard. He glanced at Eric and smiled to Trish, but otherwise paid them no more attention. Eric made a show of producing his new key to the executive elevator which whisked them up to the top floor. Eric seemed nervous while Trish was calm. She even seemed like she was looking forward to it.

"Don't worry, honey," Trish said with a smile. "I've done this a lot. It's fun fooling all those straight people."

"Well, I've never done it before!" Eric said. "I just want to get this done and over with, then take you out somewhere nice, and see if I can bring you home with me and get you drunk and have my way with you," he winked at her.

"Oh, come on Eric! You're being silly!" Trish laughed. "You know damn well you don't have to get me drunk first!"

Eric took some deep breaths and Trish gave him a peck on his cheek. "Come *on* honey, calm down! It won't be that bad! We're just gonna have a few drinks and talk a lot, right? It's not like we're going to do anything like what we did at "The Queen of Hearts," so just go with it."

The elevator doors opened into the lobby of the top floor and they walked in. Eric stumbled a little and Trish was composed. Eric's new boss walked up and Eric introduced Trish. She offered her hand and his boss took it and gave Trish the usual compliments. Then his mistress entered the room and Trish suddenly lost all composure and put a death grip on Eric's hand.

Eric was no help. It was all he and Trish could do to keep straight faces as Marlene started across the room toward them with her arms held out. Neither of them noticed that she was a blonde tonight and that she, too, was toned down and looked simply elegant in a gold, floor length, evening gown. No sashaying this time, but she seemed to glide across the room.

"Eric!" she said. "So nice to see you again! And Trish!" she gave her a quick hug. "Very nice to finally meet you!" The two of them could only stare. Marlene hooked her hand around Trish's arm and her other arm went lightly around Eric's waist. "Let's go meet the others," she smiled, and had to give them a little yank to get them started walking. Eric looked around the room and he and Trish let out a small gasp as they recognized some of the other "women" from the bar, who were all looking at them and teasing them with their smiles. Marlene said, just loud enough for the both of them to hear, "Told you I had friends that would surprise you, honey!" Eric glanced at his boss, who was watching with a twinkle in his eye, and a teasingly evil grin on his face.

Marlene looked radiant, smiling as she walked back across the room with Eric and Trish in tow on either side of her, both of them with their heads turned towards her, giving her a hard stare, and the folks one floor below who were only working late trying to get ahead just knew they were going to hear those damn noises again!

■

DOUBLE COUPON DAY

Hank normally hated grocery shopping at this hour. The time just after most folks got off work, but before usual dinnertime, was when the damn place was always so crowded. However, he did need all the stuff that filled his shopping cart, so he couldn't really complain – though he wouldn't have anyway. Not in this particular store.

The weather was going sour. Even though the clouds were rolling in and had already blocked out the sun, Hank had his shades on inside the store. He didn't care whether or not the sun was out. There was another reason he had his shades on.

He was standing in line at the checkout and it was busy. There were three other people ahead of him – all with full shopping carts. In spite of the crowds and the wait, Hank didn't grumble like most people did about the long lines and the inconsiderate customers that seemed to have fun finding new ways to hold up the line. People, for instance, like the ones who waited until the total was rung up before they even pull out their checkbook (Hank had his check already filled out except for the amount). What especially irritated Hank was the damn women who stood idly watching until the total was rung up – *then* they started fishing in their huge purses for their wallets when they should have had it out and open and ready…fucking cunts!

No, Hank didn't complain out loud. He had a way to amuse himself while waiting in line. He loved to check out the bag boys while he waited. That was the reason he was wearing his shades. He could stare at the cute guys as they worked, and no one could see where his eyes were looking. Today there was a lot of eye candy to occupy his time. This store in particular always had a great crop of young guys flitting back and forth, filling up bags and sacks, and bending over and all. Hank learned a long time ago to keep a straight face in spite of wanting to smile or make eye contact with these guys to judge their reaction. When he was a young guy himself it was fairly easy to hit on these guys. But now that he was in his 40's, he had to be careful. So Hank kept his shades on and maintained a poker face.

The store had a policy that the bag boys would walk a customer's groceries to their car and load them if the customer wanted. Usually a tip was expected, but most people these days won't part with even an extra dollar, so most of the baggers had to put up with their minimum wage. Hank saw that the lady who just finished paying did choose to have the bagger help her out to her car. When another bagger took his place at the end of the belt, Hank almost lost his composure.

He was the proverbial drop dead fucking gorgeous! Probably about 5' 6", maybe 130 pounds if that much. Jet-black hair cut short, thick eyebrows and big dark eyes. Hank didn't even try to guess his age. Teenagers can really fool you. They can look real young, yet have already graduated high school, and they can look college age, but not even be old enough to drive yet. You just can't tell with them, and you couldn't tell with this guy, either, but Hank would have guessed him to be about 19.

He had a classic chiseled face, and even though his stature was small, Hank could tell even at that distance that the kid was getting his body worked out somehow. Maybe some sports at school, maybe regular workouts, but Hank liked the way his arm muscles flexed as he loaded the groceries into bags. The baggers all wore short-sleeved white shirts with a red vest carrying the store's logo, and this kid's shirt fit him tight enough to show off some definition in his chest. They all wore black jeans, and while none of the guys wore any real tight fitting, teen slut type of jeans, this kid's pants fit just tight enough to show Hank a nice little bubble butt. Man, he was stacked!!

Now Hank only had one more customer to wait for and the bagger was still in his line. He hoped the lady in front of him didn't want the guy to take her bags to her car. Hank still eyed the guy, silently drooling inside. He noticed the kid's arms were smooth and figured his chest and butt were too. Hank had his eye on the kid's crotch. His jeans fit just right there too! He probably had a nice bush between his legs, and his bushy eyebrows presaged a hairy body in the future, but right now Hank figured there was a nice smooth body under those clothes.

All right! The lady in front of Hank pushed her own cart of bagged groceries away from the line herself! The kid looked up at Hank.

"Paper or plastic, sir?" the kid said automatically. Hank saw his nametag: "Matt." Now Hank took off his shades and looked the smiling kid in his eye.

"Plastic's fine," he smiled at Matt. Matt held his gaze only for an instant, nodded, and went to work. Hank didn't pay any attention to the cashier. He didn't pay any attention to the doors leading out of the store where flashes of lightning were frequent and a little ominous. In fact, it seemed his entire peripheral vision became blurred as he focused on watching Matt bag the groceries, and without even knowing it, show off his gorgeous body.

Matt glanced up a few times while working and caught Hank's eye, smiled quickly and kept on working. When the groceries were bagged and paid for, Matt smiled a little wider at Hank.

"Load your car for you, sir?" Matt asked with a smile but without a lot of conviction, since most people declined.

"Sure," Hank said and smiled at Matt. "I'm parked out back though. That okay?"

Matt smiled a little wider and shrugged his shoulders. "No problem, sir."

So Matt pushed the cart ahead of Hank, and Hank couldn't take his eyes off Matt's little butt straining his pants while he walked.

Outside, they were greeted with a brilliant flash of lightning immediately followed by loud and rumbling thunder.

"Wow!" Matt said and flashed Hank with another smile.

"Yeah," Hank answered, scanning the dark sky. "Looks like it'll hit any second now."

No sooner said than the first drops hit the sidewalk, and they were big ones.

"You sure you wanna load my car?" Hank laughed.

"You bet, sir." Matt said a little excitedly. Hank knew he was thinking he'd get a bigger tip. Hank swung his hand out to guide Matt to his car.

"I always park in the back," Hank told Matt while they walked. "My van is oversized, longer than most, and it won't fit in the parking spaces in front here."

"That's okay, sir," Matt answered. "Soon as I get back in I can clock out, and I really don't want to bag up even one more sack today!" He looked at Hank and smiled again, turning Hank on more and more each time he showed that sweet smile.

No sooner had they cleared the corner of the building and walked away from the protection of the roof than the sky opened up with a vengeance. They felt almost like they were standing under a shower nozzle as the rain beat down on them. Hank asked one more time if Matt wanted to forget it and go back inside before he got too wet. Matt just laughed.

"I don't care!" Matt had to almost shout now to be heard over the pouring rain and thunder. "I can get dry when I get home, but one way or the other, this is the *last* bag I fill up today!" and started to push the cart again.

Hank, laughing, grabbed the front of the cart, Matt had the back, and they both took off running. While the back parking lot wasn't all that big, it seemed like Hank's van was a mile away since the rain was beating down on them. He was parked on the other side of the parking lot and they both got soaked running across it.

Hank wrenched the back doors open, and he and Matt started literally throwing the bags into the back. As they unloaded the cart they both laughed at how wet they were getting, and suddenly the wind picked up. Now the rain was being driven sideways and the lightning became almost continuous. As the last bag flew into the van, a bolt of lightning struck a nearby tree, and Hank and Matt both felt vibrations in their bodies when the sound hit them. They both instinctively ducked a little at the flash and the noise. The wind picked up even more and the van was rocking a little.

"Jump in!" Hank yelled to Matt. "We can wait it out inside!" Matt didn't argue, but dove into the back of the van followed closely by Hank, who slammed the doors behind him.

"Whew!" Matt said. "I didn't expect *this* much." He held his arms up. His sleeves and his vest were dripping water.

"Yeah!" Hank said. "Almost like a damn tornado, eh?" He was as wet as Matt, and they looked at each other and laughed. Matt grabbed a corner of his vest and squeezed a little water out.

"Fucking soaked!" he exclaimed and then shot a glance at Hank and put his hand up to his mouth. "Oh! Sorry, sir!" he said through his hand.

Hank reached over and flicked Matt's name tag, "Oh, hell, don't worry about it, Matt," he smiled. "I'm fucking soaked too!"

Matt looked around the van. It was long enough to hold five rows of seats, much like a hotel van, but there was only the driver's and one passenger seat. The rest of the van was customized, with a higher roof, and ready for a man to stand up in, and live in.

"Wow!" he said, wide-eyed, to Hank. "This is some ride, sir!"

Hank laughed. "Looks like we may be stuck here for a while, Matt," Hank said as the wind continued to rock the van. "How 'bout you drop the 'sir'. Name's Hank," he said and shook Matt's hand.

Matt was right about the van: Along the wall on the passenger side, in place of a window, was some shelves and cabinets, a tiny sink, a small refrigerator, and a two-burner stove. There was even a battery-operated heater on the floor, connected to a register running along the whole wall. Hank explained that he liked to travel, and sleeping in the van saved a lot of money.

Hank rose up on his knees in front of Matt, and smoothly pulled his t-shirt off. He noticed that Matt's eyes immediately went to his chest. Hank didn't look bad for his age. He wasn't fat, didn't have a whole lot of gray hair, and even still had a full head of hair. He worked out regularly, and had a nice pair of pecs, with a moderately thick mat of hair going from one nipple to the next, culminating in a trail running down into his pants.

Hank rose up and spread his shirt out over the heating register and turned on the heater. He looked at Matt and saw that Matt's eyes were still on his chest. He smiled. "Go ahead and take off your shirt, Matt. We can start it drying a little on the register here while I warm up this thing."

Matt hesitated a little, glanced out the window of the van to see that the rain showed no sign of letting up. He shrugged his shoulders and took off his vest. Hank took Matt's vest and put it on a small hanger he got from one the cabinets and hung it up on the cabinet door.

Matt kept glancing at Hank as he unbuttoned his shirt. He pulled it off a little shyly, confirming Hank's prediction that his chest was both smooth and pretty well defined. Hank took his shirt and spread it out on the register.

Hank ducked again when another bolt of lightning hit something close by and wound up lying down while the thunder rolled and they both laughed. Then Hank very calmly kicked his shoes off and unzipped his pants. He glanced over at Matt, who was watching Hank, as his eyes got a little bigger. Hank just smiled at Matt while he tugged his soaked pants down, showing his cock outlined in his wet briefs. Matt glanced over at Hank's body. His smile stayed on his face.

"Hell, Matt, it's just us in here," Hank told him. "Go ahead and strip down. I got some towels around here somewhere. We can at least get dry and warm for now." Hank finished pulling his wet jeans off, reached up and spread them out on the register, too. He looked at Matt, who hadn't moved yet and was staring at the window while the rain blotted out all vision. Hank smiled at Matt's nervousness.

"See?" he told Matt. "No one can see, and you'll get damn cold sitting there wet like that. Go on Matt, it's okay."

Matt sat up another second then shrugged his shoulders again. "Well, okay."

Hank turned to open a cabinet for some towels and his cock stirred when he heard Matt's zipper behind him. He grabbed some towels and tossed a couple onto Matt's chest while Matt struggled with his pants.

"Here, let me help," Hank said and grabbed the cuffs of Matt's pants.

"That's okay! I can do it!" Matt said suddenly, even apprehensively, but Hank already had a hold of both cuffs and pulled. He pulled so hard that he pulled Matt along the floor a little and Matt wound up falling back and smacking his head on the floor.

"Oh shit! Sorry, Matt!" Hank laughed.

Matt giggled a little. "'s okay," he said, and scissored his legs while Hank pulled his pants, shoes, and socks the rest of the way off.

Matt picked up a towel and started drying himself off. Hank reached over the driver's seat and flipped a switch that turned on a light inside the van. Now he could look back from behind Matt and see his dick outlined in his wet underwear. Hank silently whistled to himself and had to consciously not smack his lips at the nice package Matt had tucked into those little briefs.

Hank returned to his knees in front of Matt and started toweling himself off. He noticed Matt sneaking glances at his body, and took some time rubbing the towel across his chest to give Matt a little show. Then he calmly hooked his thumbs in the waistband of his briefs and pushed them down, letting his cock flop out.

Matt shot a look at Hank and sucked in a breath, "Uh, sir..." he started to say, but Hank just laughed.

"Aw, come on, Matt," Hank said. "It's getting cold in here being all wet. Don't tell me you never saw a naked man before?"

Matt just shook his head, and tried to look away, but Hank saw his eyes glancing at his cock.

"Well, the guys at school of course. But this isn't a locker room." Matt looked out the window again, even though there was nothing to see but the rain running down the glass.

Hank laughed again and clapped Matt on his shoulder. Matt jumped a little at the contact but didn't say anything. Hank kept on talking.

"Hell, Matt, this thing is like my second home. I'm always naked at home, and when I'm holed up inside here, I'm always naked here too. Besides, neither of us has anything to hide. I just want ya to be comfortable, and it's impossible to get comfortable wet like this. Go ahead and hang your shorts on the heater. No one will come in here and no one needs to know there's a couple of naked guys in here." Hank had every reason to be confident, as Matt would find out later.

Matt smiled a little. "Sure," he said. He leaned back and raised his little butt off the floor. Hank's eyes half closed as Matt slid his briefs down his legs, sat up and pulled them off. Hank almost reached down to grab his own cock as Matt got up on his knees to put his briefs up on the register. He had, as Hank hoped, a nice smooth, tight little bubble butt. Hank caught that Matt took a few extra seconds more than was necessary to hang his shorts up, giving Hank a little extra time to admire his beautiful ass. When Matt sat back down against the back of the front seat, his dick was already stirring.

Hank rolled up on his side and turned to the refrigerator. When he opened the door he glanced behind him and caught Matt checking out his butt. He only asked, "How 'bout a soda? Or I got some orange juice, too."

"Thanks," Matt said, his voice a little quiet. "Soda would be good."

Hank handed Matt a can. Matt opened it, took a sip, and then held the can down between his legs, letting his hands cover his dick.

Hank got a can for himself then turned back over so he was lying on his back, his cock lying off to one side right next to Matt, who tried not to look at it. Hank smiled at the glances Matt was giving it. It took all of Hank's concentration not to pop a boner right then and there.

"You play some kind of sports in school, don't ya?" he asked Matt.

"I ran track in high school," Matt said simply and took another sip of his soda.

"Yeah," Hank told him, "you look like you've got a fine runner's body going." That got him another nervous glance. "Bet you got a bunch of trophies, don't ya?"

Matt shook his head. "No," he said still without looking at Hank. "Just some certificates. I wasn't that good."

Hank laid back and looked at Matt's smooth back. "I ran track in school too," he told Matt.

That earned him a direct look from Matt who turned with a tiny smile at the corners of his mouth. "Yeah?"

"Sure did," Hank answered. "But I only got one trophy, and *that* was only for third place!" he laughed.

Matt snickered a little. "That's about how I did!" he told Hank.

Now that they had some common ground, Matt loosened up a little. Hank thought Matt would ask him to cover his cock with a towel, but he didn't. Hank kept a smile on his face while they talked.

They talked about track and sports and how Matt was doing in college. Worst subjects, favorite subject, career plans – usual stuff. Matt loosened up a little more and asked questions about the van, and Hank told him he'd done most of the work himself, little by little. They talked and drank their soda and eventually Matt turned around some and was now looking directly at Hank while they talked. Hank cracked some jokes and Matt laughed. Soon Matt was leaning up against the back of the driver's seat while Hank was against the passenger's seat as the storm wore on.

Then Hank asked Matt if he had a girlfriend.

Once again Matt's eyes lowered a little. "Nah," he said. "Not right now."

"Really?" Hank asked. "I'd think a guy like you wouldn't be hurtin'. You look great, you're an athlete, you're smart, and a hard worker, I can see. You'd be a good catch I'd think."

Then Hank took the plunge.

"Do you like girls, Matt?" he asked softly.

Matt's whole body stiffened perceptibly. "Well, yeah," he said but in a small voice, once again not looking at Hank, and Hank had his answer.

Hank rolled on his side to face Matt. He waited a few seconds, then smiled and asked, softly again, "Do you like guys?"

Matt's head snapped up and his eyes widened. He opened his mouth but no sound came out immediately. Hank didn't move, but just smiled.

"Hey, Matt," he said, "it's okay. It sure didn't used to be – not when I was in school for sure, but it's okay these days. At least it's a lot better than it used to be."

Matt's eyes closed. He took in a couple of breaths. "Well..." he opened his eyes and looked right into Hank's. "Yeah."

Hank flashed a big smile. "Cool," was all he said.

Matt kept his eyes on Hank. "So, you're gay?" he asked.

"What you mean," Hank teased him, "is that I'm gay...too."

Matt snickered a little. "Yeah, I guess that's what I mean."

"You've never told anyone before, have ya?"

Matt shook his head.

"Well, it's perfectly safe telling me," Hank told him and looked right in Matt's eyes. "I'm gay too, Matt. We're both gay."

Matt's smile loosened up some, Hank noticed. Became more real, more natural. A little more relaxed, Hank was glad to see. He pushed a little further.

"So I take it you don't have a boyfriend, then?"

Again Matt just shook his head.

"Have you done anything with any guys before? Jack off together? Maybe jack each other off?"

"No," Matt said, "I haven't done anything with anyone at all." He looked at Hank, his eyes kind of looking for some kind of approval, or encouragement. "I want to, ya know? But I get scared of getting caught and everyone finding out."

"Yeah," Hank said. "I know what you mean, Matt. There are still some people I'm not out to. A hell of a lot of people, come to think of it. Just some of my friends and most of them are gay, too. But still, most of the straight world doesn't know."

"I keep thinking," Matt told him, "that I should tell my folks at least. But my dad would lose it. I don't know what my mom would do. I always chicken out."

"You know, Matt," Hank was still on his side, his head resting on one hand. He reached out with his other hand and took hold of Matt's hand. Matt didn't resist. "There's no rule anywhere that says you're obligated to tell anyone. The problems caused by coming out are not your problems. They're everyone else's. My own feeling," Hank continued, "is that it's not my job to tell everyone I'm gay. It's their damn job to not worry about it. So I won't tell anyone unless they ask me. And hell, most of the heteros are too damn gutless to ask, so it's never been a problem for me. You tell people only if you want to. You're the boss, not them."

Matt took a deep breath, sighed and smiled at Hank. "That's easy for you to say. You're not a college kid still living at home, with your parents paying the bills!"

"I know," Hank smiled. "Parents are something else entirely. You know yours a lot better'n me, buddy, so I can't tell ya what to do with them right now. I'm certainly not gonna tell ya to rush right home and tell 'em!"

Now Matt laughed, and shook his head enthusiastically. "I wouldn't do it any way!" he laughed. He was a lot more relaxed now.

They both got quiet. The sound of the rain pounding on the van's metal roof was loud. The lightning continued to flash one bolt after another, and the thunder drowned out the sound of the rain for a few seconds.

The wind was still shaking the van while two naked guys hung out inside. Hank's eyes traveled down Matt's body to his dick. Matt was looking straight ahead. Hank slowly but smoothly let go of Matt's hand, and reached over and cupped Matt's cock and balls.

Matt sucked in a breath. He didn't really make noise, but let his breath out in one long "Hooooo!" He didn't reach to move Hank's hand away, though. Hank wrapped his hand around Matt's dick and squeezed it a little. Matt's mouth opened and he licked his lips.

His breathing picked up but he still didn't say anything. Hank could feel Matt's dick respond. Matt's muscles tightened up – his legs flinched – his toes flared. His eyes half closed and his mouth stayed open. His chest expanded noticeably as he breathed. Hank started to slowly stroke Matt's dick while it got harder. In no time it was rock hard. Matt's balls were moving around in their sac of their own accord. He was just breathing and watching Hank's hand as it slid up and down the shaft.

Hank leaned over a little closer to Matt. "Feel good, Matt?"

Matt moaned a little. Hank almost didn't hear it.

"essssssss..."

Hank asked softly, "Do you want me to stop?"

Immediately Matt shook his head. As an answer, he reached over and tentatively wrapped his hand around Hank's now hard cock. Hank almost lost it, but managed to hold back. Matt just held Hank's cock in his hand while Hank slowly jacked Matt's.

"Go ahead," Hank whispered in Matt's ear. "Squeeze it if ya want. Stroke it like I'm doin' yours if ya want."

Matt's hand started moving up and down Hank's shaft. Hank picked up the pace on Matt's dick. Now they were both jacking each other off, and it was obvious by the look on Matt's face that he was loving it. Hank didn't say anything else but silently worked Matt's dick. He doubted Matt realized what he was doing, but he started slowly bucking his hips and slow fucking Hank's hand. Hank just let Matt do whatever his young body told him to do.

On their own, Matt's hips picked up the pace. Matt's head started moving side to side. His own hand started stroking Hank's cock faster, squeezing it harder. "Oh God!" Matt moaned. He wasn't looking at Hank. Hell, his eyes weren't really focused on anything. "Oh God! Oh God!" he moaned and whispered over and over again as his hips made his dick fuck Hank's hand faster and faster. As Hank suspected, Matt couldn't hold back.

The first squirt went straight up in the air. Hank lowered Matt's dick and the second squirt splat right on Matt's own chin. Matt whimpered and huffed as squirt after squirt landed on his chest and belly and Hank kept right on jacking Matt's dick. Matt's own hand left Hank's cock and he pushed both hands on the floor while he came. His mouth was open wide but only air came out. His eyes closed and he just huffed while he came until he was done.

—

After a few seconds, Matt opened his eyes and looked into Hank's. His lips spread into a wide grin. Hank let go of Matt's dick and brought his cum-covered hand up to his lips. His tongue flicked out while Matt watched and lapped up the cum. Matt was mesmerized at the sight. He stayed silent but his eyes followed Hank's every move as Hank licked all of Matt's cum off of his hand, constantly smiling at Matt, the two faces only inches apart.

"Oh God!" was all Matt could say.

"Feels better, doesn't it," Hank whispered, "when you don't have to do it yourself?" Matt just smiled and licked his lips yet again.

As close as their faces were, Hank had only to purse his lips and they brushed up against Matt's. Then Hank did it again. Then one more time and now his lips stayed on Matt's.

It was almost the same with all virgins: once they decide to go for it, no one can match their eagerness. They give and take and give and take with wild abandon. Matt melted into Hank's arms and he sucked Hank's tongue up into his own mouth, tasting his own cum. His arms flew around Hank and his own tongue found its own way into Hank's waiting mouth, licking and sliding and flicking and exploring. Hank let him do whatever he wanted.

Matt wrapped a leg around Hank and their cocks slammed into each other's. Matt's butt cheeks flexed and relaxed and flexed as he ground his cock into Hank's. Small grunts and moans escaped his lips as he discovered what he could do with his body. Hank went with whatever Matt did or wanted done. They rolled and Matt was on top of Hank then Hank wound up on top of Matt. When Matt was on top of Hank, mashing his cock into Hank's, his whole body suddenly froze with every muscle he had taut, as he shot another load of cum over both their cocks.

Hank rolled them both over so he was on top of Matt. He slid a hand up to Matt's face and slid a finger in Matt's mouth. Matt sucked on it while Hank started slowly scooting his body down Matt's, his tongue licking all the way. Matt lay still while Hank let his tongue explore the young smooth body under him. He kissed Matt's neck and chest; licked his nipples and Matt whimpered. Hank let Matt watch him slowly lick up the cum Matt had shot on his own chest. His tongue worked its way further down and was at Matt's belly button while his fingers were still in Matt's mouth.

Hank slid further down and looked up at Matt. "Feels good?" he asked.

"Yesss. Oh God yessss." Hank barely heard him.

—

Matt felt Hank's tongue lick the inside of his thigh and he automatically spread his legs. He kept closing and opening his eyes. He wasn't sure what he was supposed to do, but had an idea that it didn't matter. What was being done to him, and what he was feeling, was way better than anything he had ever thought. He felt Hank's tongue on his other thigh, and found himself wishing Hank would do something – anything – with his dick. Just as he was about to open his mouth and beg, he felt Hank's tongue lick his dick from the base to the tip and he let out another whimper and arched his hips up he didn't know how far. His breath was coming out in waves and he sucked it back in and moaned and squirmed as waves of pleasure he'd never known before hit his crotch, spread out, and slammed into his head and toes.

Hank was between Matt's legs, which Matt had wrapped around him like he never intended to let Hank go. Typical of teenagers, Matt's dick was still hard in spite of cumming twice in quick succession. While Hank licked the last of the cum off of it, Matt reached down without looking, grabbed his own dick and held it straight up. Hank swallowed it whole and Matt almost yelled. Hank sucked and sucked on that young meat and Matt whimpered and sucked harder on Hank's fingers. Hank sucked just as hard on Matt's dick and grabbed his thigh and took all of that meat in his mouth while his tongue swirled up and down and all around it while it was in his mouth.

Hank pulled his fingers out of Matt's mouth and Matt kept on moaning and whimpering with his eyes closed. His own hands moved by themselves up to his nipples and played with them while Hank went nuts on that dick. Hank started playing with Matt's balls while he sucked, and before he knew it, Matt was shooting his third load of cum down Hank's throat. Hank swallowed and gulped and sucked Matt's dick dry. Hank smiled inwardly at the vitality of youth as he realized it took three loads of cum in the space of less than 10 minutes, but he finally felt Matt's dick start to soften in his mouth…a little.

Now Matt opened his eyes and looked down his body at Hank sucking the last drops of cum into his mouth. Hank looked up, saw Matt and climbed back up Matt's body to kiss him. Matt locked his arms around Hank and drew their lips together, hungrily licking his cum back off Hank's tongue and inside his mouth.

After a long kiss, Matt broke away and looked right into Hank's eyes. He took a breath and said, "I wanna suck yours!"

Hank acted like he was going to say something, but Matt rolled them over and couldn't crawl down Hank's body fast enough. Hank just lay back, watched and smiled. Matt got his face right over Hank's cock and grabbed hold of it. Eager as he was, Matt was still a little tentative.

His tongue flicked out and quickly licked the pre-cum off Hank's cock. Matt's lips smacked a few times as he tested the taste of Hank's cock and pre-cum. Then his mouth opened wide and swallowed the head of Hank's cock. Hank let his head fall back and relaxed. He knew a first timer had to try things out first, so he didn't do anything to hurry Matt up. It felt good anyway.

Matt kept his mouth wide open and shoved as much of Hank's cock in as he could. His lips closed and his cheeks sunk in as he put a suck on his first cock. Hank moaned encouragement as Matt's mouth started working up and down Hank's shaft. Hank was moaning sincerely now and reached down and ran his fingers through Matt's hair, gently guiding Matt's head up and down. Hank kept on encouraging Matt with some, "Yeahs," and a, "That's it. That's how you do it," now and then, but mostly Matt was doing just fine on his own. He sucked Hank's cock and licked the shaft from base to head. His mouth dove into Hank's sac and he sucked Hank's balls up into his mouth one at a time.

Hank reached down to Matt, told him to keep on sucking, which Matt did without a word. Hank maneuvered Matt's body around until he straddled Hank. Hank reached up and pulled Matt's hard again dick down and stuffed it into his mouth. Both of them sucked dick and moaned, and the storm wore on, but neither noticed.

Hank's hands reached up and played with Matt's butt. He squeezed the cheeks and ran his fingers up and down the crack. Matt started whimpering again and moved his little butt in rhythm with Hank's strokes. Hank let Matt's dick flop out of his mouth. He put his hands on Matt's hips and pushed him slightly forward and pulled him down. Matt was still sucking like crazy on Hank's cock, but let it fall out of his mouth and almost howled like a dog at the moon when Hank's tongue raked across his virgin fuckhole.

"Oh God!!" seemed to be all Matt could think to say. He instinctively started rocking his body back and forth as Hank worked his tongue all over that sweet little ass. Every thrust of his tongue into Matt's butt seemed to push a breath out of Matt, who could only rock back and forth and enjoy. Hank was feeling pretty good himself! He was having a blast eating out that young butt, and his own body had trouble lying still.

Matt was moaning and whimpering, and now and then would quickly lick Hank's cock. Matt had trouble sucking on it though, because he kept stopping to moan. Hank spread his legs wide and started to wrap them around Matt. Matt took it as some kind of sign and leaned over, stuck his tongue out, and just like a virgin, gave Hank's ass a quick lick.

That was all it took, and suddenly Matt's whole face was buried in Hank's ass, and the two of them started a great butt licking 69, and the van rocked on with the wind, and the two naked guys inside ate each other's butts. The noise they made was fortunately drowned out by the storm.

Matt's butt was good and wet and slippery now. Hank reached up and took a finger and started rubbing Matt's little hole. It took a while, but with a little pressure at first, slowly increasing, Hank's finger suddenly slid inside Matt's hole and Matt almost lifted his whole body up off Hank's.

"Ooh yeah!" Matt mumbled, and sat very still while Hank worked his finger in and out of Matt's ass, now and then flicking his tongue out for a quick lick. Before Matt knew what Hank was doing, Hank worked a second finger up Matt's chute, which made Matt moan even louder. Matt's ass was tight all right, and Hank thought the circulation in his fingers was being cut off. Without taking his fingers out of Matt's ass, Hank maneuvered around until Matt was lying on his stomach on the floor. Hank was on his knees beside Matt, and leaned over to eat his butt some more, finger fuck it some more, eat it some more, finger fuck it until he felt Matt's hole loosen up and stay relaxed. Hank smiled as he looked down and admired the beautiful young body on the floor while he finger fucked Matt's tight little butt.

He leaned down to whisper in Matt's ear, "We don't have to if you don't want to, Matt," Hank said as he wiggled his fingers inside Matt's ass to show what he meant.

Matt turned his head to look at Hank. His eyes were glazed over, and not really looking directly at Hank, just in his general direction.

"I want it, Hank," he mumbled. "Fuck me! Go ahead and fuck me, Hank. I want it so bad. I want it right now!"

Hank leaned down further and kissed Matt quickly. "You got it, Matt," was all he said. He reached into one of the cabinets and grabbed a tube of lube. He squirted some on Matt's ass and Matt bucked a little at the coldness. Now Hank's fingers worked the lube up into Matt's ass while Hank tore open a condom and rolled it down his cock. He got between Matt's wide spread legs and lowered himself down and his cock seemed to find Matt's hole by itself.

Hank leaned forward again and started whispering into Matt's ear, telling him how to get ready, what to do when his ass was penetrated, all the while slowly but surely increasing the pressure his cock was putting against Matt's hole.

Just as the head of his cock popped into Matt's virgin butt, Matt's head snapped up and he sucked in a huge gulp of air. He didn't say anything, but Hank saw his eyes squint and his teeth bare as he sucked in gulp after gulp of air.

Hank slowly pushed some of his cock into Matt's ass and pulled back. He waited a few seconds then slid more of his cock up Matt's ass and pulled back. He worked slowly, all the while watching Matt's face. Finally he saw Matt's squinted eyes relax so he pushed even more of his cock in. Matt took it all fine, and soon was breathing normally again and even let his face fall back on the floor. After a couple of minutes, his lips spread into a smile.

Hank knew things were good now. So he picked up the pace. He still whispered into Matt's ear, telling him he was doing fine, better than most, that he felt good, that he was a great fuck, and finally he felt Matt's hips respond as they started to buck a little, meeting Hank's cock with each thrust.

Hank rose up a little and braced himself up on his hands. Now he could look down and watch his cock and hips work Matt's little butt. He couldn't help it now, and since he knew Matt felt fine he started to shove his cock in harder. Now Matt's little butt cheeks started to jiggle a little as Hank fucked and slammed into them.

"How is it, Matt?" Hank asked with a smile in his voice. "You're gettin' fucked now, buddy!" and he picked up the pace even more, and soon no one could tell if the van was rocking only from the storm. Hank reached and passed the proverbial point of no return, and started fucking Matt's ass with wild abandon. Grunting and huffing and working up a sweat in the warm van, Hank fucked away on that young butt and both of them were grunting with each thrust. Matt's only answer to Hank's words was more grunts and whimpers, but always with a smile. Hank could tell by the way Matt's butt cheeks tightened up that he was shooting yet another load of cum, and Hank kept right on fucking Matt.

Hank suddenly pulled his cock out of Matt's ass, grabbed Matt and flipped him over on his back. Matt's legs spread all on their own and his feet went up in the air. Hank quickly stuck his cock back into Matt's hole and fucked away. Sure enough, as Hank looked down he could see fresh cum on Matt's cock. He worked his way up to his knees and reached down and stroked Matt's still hard dick while he fucked. Matt's whimpering turned into moans of pleasure synchronized with Hank's thrusts. Hank grabbed Matt's ankles and pushed his legs even further apart. He looked down and watched his cock slide in and out of Matt's little ass and that made him fuck even harder.

Matt alternated between opening his eyes to look down his body to try to see the cock that was fucking him, and closing his eyes and letting his head fall back. He started cheering Hank on, now fully enthralled at what was happening to him. Some "Yesss's" and some "Don't stop's" and some "Fuck me's" made their way out of his mouth but he didn't seem to realize he was saying them.

Matt reached down and started jacking his own cock and Hank leaned down. His lips touched Matt's. Both mouths opened and tongues did battle. Their sweat mingled and their bodies slid over each other. Matt had his legs wrapped around Hank tight, almost as though he was using them to push Hank into his ass even harder. Hank's butt cheeks tightened and relaxed as he drilled Matt's hole and ground his hips and sucked on Matt's tongue. Hank knew he was going to lose it and just let it happen.

Matt's butt worked instinctively and milked the cum out of Hank's cock, and both of them felt Matt's cum shooting between them. Matt's mouth formed an "O" and stayed there while he came. His eyes rolled back in his head and his cock pumped by itself. Hank huffed and puffed and filled the condom full of cum. He slowly pulled his cock out of Matt's ass, pulled the condom off and let his cum pour out of it to mix with Matt's own cum on his chest and belly. Matt kept his legs spread and his feet up in the air, and whimpered while Hank lapped up the cum on Matt. He leaned forward and Matt opened his mouth. They passed the cum back and forth and back and forth until it dissolved. Hank half laid, half fell to Matt's side. Both bodies were sweaty and wet and sticky. Both had a smile on their faces.

Hank snickered a little and had to reach out and gently push Matt's legs back down to the floor. Matt then rolled over and snuggled into Hank's body. Hank almost didn't hear Matt's whispered, "Thank you!" but that was okay. He just held Matt for a while, stroking his hair and whispering how good he was. The windows were steamed over and it was warm in the van. The two naked guys lay together and hugged and kissed and didn't care where they were.

"Hey," Hank said.

"Yeah?" came the muffled question as Matt had his face buried in Hank's chest.

"The storm stopped," Hank said.

"What storm?" Matt asked and they both chuckled.

The storm had indeed stopped. There was only the sound of a light drizzle now. Hank poured some water in the tiny sink and they both washed up some. Their clothes weren't really dry but Matt had to get home so they got dressed. He said he'd just tell his folks he ran home in the rain, but that they probably wouldn't notice him coming in anyway.

They got in the front of the van and Hank drove Matt home, both totally forgetting that Matt hadn't gone back into the store to clock out.

On the way, Matt gave Hank his work schedule for the next couple of weeks. They kissed one more time near Matt's house, then he slid out of the van and went on home.

Hank did quite a bit of shopping the next couple of weeks. At least he was at the store a lot. He'd get there a few minutes before Matt was due to get off work and would wait in the back of the van. Matt would run out after work, and the two of them would go at it in the van for a while.

Matt was a quick learner, and soon was jumping on Hank's cock and fucking himself with it while he bounced up and down, and Hank loved it. It didn't take long for them to start also meeting at Hank's house. Matt got good at teasing and turning Hank on. He'd walk into Hank's house and sometimes immediately strip down and parade in front of Hank with his hard cock swinging back and forth. He'd find excuses to turn around and bend over to give Hank a good look at his butt. Other times he'd undress languidly, often getting on his knees with just his jeans on, then making a show of unzipping them real slow in front of Hank until his cock popped out. He'd leer at Hank and jack his cock for a while on his knees before he took his jeans the rest of the way off. And sometimes he'd just jump on Hank and kiss him deep and wet and dirty, and they'd almost rip each other's clothes off and just plain ole fuck.

Matt was getting very good at taking a cock up his ass, and told Hank that he'd even met another guy from his school and was fucking around with him. He told Hank he'd told his new buddy that he was fucking an older guy, and at first his buddy thought it was gross, but seemed to be changing his mind as Matt talked about the fun they had. He grinned at Hank, knowing he was teasing about the possibility of bringing his buddy over. They fucked all over Hank's house, in every room, and Matt eventually bent over every piece of furniture. He took Hank's cock up his butt fast or slow, rode it like a cowboy, rocked back and forth on his hands and knees, and backed Hank up against a wall and bent over and fucked himself with Hank's cock while Hank was trapped against the wall.

Hank figured it was time to give Matt his surprise, and so, one day after dropping Matt off near his house, he went home and made a phone call.

About a week later, Hank saw Matt at the grocery store again. This time Hank really did have some groceries to buy. As usual, he'd made sure he went through the checkout just before Matt was due to get off work. Matt wasn't bagging groceries in Hank's line, but Hank walked past him on his way out of the store. They made eye contact for just a second, but Matt nodded and flashed Hank his sexy smile, and Hank answered with a quick wink of his eye. That was their signal that Hank would be waiting in his van in the back parking lot again.

Also as usual, he didn't have to wait long. Matt was one horny little fucker when he ran across the parking lot and jumped into the back of the van. Hank was waiting for him naked. Matt managed to kick his shoes off and get out of his vest and shirt while putting a hell of a suck on Hank's cock. Hank reached out and unzipped Matt's pants, feeling his rock hard cock through the material. He played with Matt's cock a bit then pulled his pants off for him. Matt wasn't wearing underwear that day (another thing he did now and then to tease Hank), so it only took seconds for Matt to climb up on top of Hank and jam his butt down on Hank's face, all the while without taking his mouth off Hank's cock.

He did start to moan when he first felt a finger from each of Hank's hands work their way into his hole and stretch it out a bit, then he almost hollered out loud as Hank's tongue slid up his ass and licked him from the inside. Hank loved eating out a tight little butt and Matt fit that bill perfectly. Hank's tongue in his ass made Matt suck harder and his spit was running down Hank's balls.

Matt kept up with it and lapped Hank's balls and sucked them into his mouth one at a time. Soon Hank's legs were spread and Matt was leaning forward and eating Hank's ass while Hank munched away on Matt's. They hadn't said a word to each other yet, but just went at it.

Hank could tell by the way Matt was bucking his hips and trembling that he was about to shoot his first load. Matt suddenly scooted up, grabbed Hank's cock, stood it up straight, and sat right down on it and started bouncing up and down on it while Hank watched his back muscles and butt cheeks. After only a couple of minutes Matt jumped off Hank's cock, turned around and sat on his chest, jacking his cock furiously. Finally some noise was made as Matt grunted and hooted while he shot a nice load of cum on Hank's face and in his mouth. Hank just laid back and swallowed and licked and smiled. He reached up and Matt fell into his arms, stretched out his body on top of Hank, and started lapping his cum off Hank's face. Now and then he'd scoop some cum on his tongue and feed it to Hank and they'd make out and taste Matt's cum together.

After Matt caught his breath he pulled his tongue out of Hank's mouth and sat up on Hank's chest. He smiled his teaser smile at Hank and rubbed his still hard cock slowly over Hank's face. Hank gave it a quick lick or kiss as it passed over his lips.

"Guess what?" Matt asked, still smiling and rubbing his cock on Hank's face.

"What?" Hank played the game.

"My buddy wants to join us. He told me just today."

"Yeah?" Hank smiled now. "Bring him on!"

"I can bring him over sometime, or we can meet right here in the van," Matt told him.

"But how will he know when to be here?" Hank asked. He reached up and started rubbing Matt's chest as they talked.

"I'll just bring him with me." Matt smiled. "He works here too."

"No kiddin'!" Hank was real interested now. "I've probably seen him then. Which one is he?"

Matt shook his head. "He's not a bagger," he said. "He works in the back with the deliveries and stuff. He hardly comes out front except to go on break. His name's Corey. He's so hot, Hank!" Matt was rubbing his cock a little harder now at the thought. "He's blonde with blue eyes, and he makes me so fuckin' horny all the time. I can't wait to watch you fuck him."

Hank was starting to squirm a little at the thought. Now Matt was actively stroking his cock right over Hank's face while he described Corey. Hank listened and started looking a little puzzled. Matt noticed and asked what was wrong.

"Oh, nothing!" Hank answered quickly. "I – uh – I was just wondering how you found out he's gay and all." Hank swallowed hard.

"Oh, don't worry!" Matt said quickly. "I really didn't know. He came on to me – in the break room!"

"Wow!" Hank laughed. "He's got guts."

"Yeah," Matt giggled. "We were just talking about stuff and hanging out on break, ya know? Somebody left the room and we were alone." Matt shrugged his shoulders "Suddenly he just reached under the table and grabbed my crotch. He leaned into me and told me he wanted to suck my dick! I almost jumped right outta my chair!"

They laughed, but then Hank got a little serious. "He's okay isn't he? I mean, is he open about being gay? Will others start talking about you if they see you hanging out with him? That could get back to your folks you know. You shouldn't let that happen until you're ready, and this town isn't all that big."

"Oh no, don't worry about that," Matt was squirming on Hank's chest now. "He's real straight acting. He's bi and has a girlfriend and all, so no one suspects." Matt looked behind him out the window. He looked back at Hank and jerked his thumb toward the store behind him, "He's there now," he told Hank. "He gets off in a few minutes. I can go in and get him if you want." Obviously Matt was real excited about the idea. His cock was even harder than it was when he first came in the van.

But Hank suddenly stiffened up a little. "Uh," he said and swallowed hard again, "maybe we'd better wait a bit, buddy."

Matt looked confused. "What's wrong, Hank? He's okay, really he is. He won't tell anyone or anything."

"Oh, it's not that," Hank said quickly. "I'd love to get him in here naked with us. It's just that…well…Maybe we'd better pick another day…you know…so I can make sure I'm ready and got time and all." He looked at Matt and Matt saw Hank looked worried. He reached down and put his fingers on Hank's lips.

"Well, okay Hank, if ya wanna," Matt said, a little disappointed. "But, I kinda told him we could maybe do it today, ya know. I didn't think you'd mind. He'll be leaving any minute now." Matt turned around to look out the back window and suddenly his whole body froze.

"What is it?" Hank asked and started to sit up.

"Awww SHIT!" Matt yelled.

"What? What?" Hank asked and tried to get out from under Matt. Matt suddenly jumped off Hank and fell off to the side.

"Oh FUCK!" he yelled again. "It's my fuckin' boss! He's heading right for us!!"

Hank relaxed a little but Matt became a blur in the van trying to gather up his clothes. It didn't really work since his clothes were all over the van where he and Hank had tossed them. Hank made no move to reach for his own clothes, but reached out and tried to calm Matt down.

That didn't work either. Matt was trying to put his shirt on, but of course the sleeves were inside out and he just wasn't getting anywhere. "He'll fire my ass! Oh, shit, Hank! He'll tell my folks an…ohhh no!" Matt's face had lost all its color, and he looked to Hank like he was about to pass out from fright. Hank didn't have time to do anything. Matt suddenly remembered that when he'd jumped in the van and slammed the door shut, he hadn't locked it. He made a lunge to the door to try to flick the lock down.

He almost made it, too.

But not quite. Just as he made his lunge, the back door was wrenched open, and instead of locking the door, Matt's own momentum made him fly naked right into his boss's arms. His boss caught Matt as he was halfway out the door, almost ready to fall right out of the van and roll his naked body on the concrete of the parking lot, right out in the open.

"Whoa there, boy!" his boss's voice boomed out. Matt had simply gone limp in his boss's arms. His boss eased the naked body back into the van. "You better git back inside here, Matt!" His boss was laughing. "You don't need to put on any shows right here in the parking lot!"

Matt almost fell backwards and couldn't even look his boss in the eye. He curled up into a fetal position and tried to cover his cock with his hands. His boss climbed up into the van and slammed the door shut, still laughing. He looked at Hank. "You weren't kiddin' about this boy, were ya Hank?" he asked.

Now Matt's eyes looked up at Hank. Hank thought he hadn't seen Matt's eyes so big. He couldn't help but smile himself. He looked at Matt's boss. "Not at all, George! He's everything I said he was."

George's booming laugh filled the van. Hank was looking at Matt and trying hard not to break out laughing himself. At least, not yet. He had a finger up to his mouth and was looking at Matt like he was waiting for Matt to explode.

"What the...!" Matt looked from Hank to George and back and forth again. Finally, Hank let out a little laugh. He reached out and pulled Matt to him, which made Matt's body uncurl so that his cock was back out in the open. Hank wrapped his arms around Matt and pulled Matt's head into his chest.

"Hell Matt!" Hank told him while snickering. "Don't worry buddy – it's okay. Really it is. Ole George here is an old fuck buddy of mine."

Matt pulled away from Hank and his eyes bore into Hank's. "Ah shit!" he yelled. "Aw bullshit!"

George was almost doubled up laughing. Hank just put his finger back up to his mouth and squinted his eyes waiting for Matt's next outburst.

None of the color had returned to Matt's face yet. He just sat there in something of a daze with his legs slightly spread, his cock now limp and laying off to one side. His balls almost all but vanished as they shrunk up under his cock like they were trying to hide there. Matt was still looking back and forth between the two men. His mouth was dropped open but no sound was coming out. He noticed that his boss was still laughing almost hysterically while looking at Hank, who wasn't sure whether or not he could get away with laughing, so just stared wide eyed at Matt with his finger still up to his mouth.

Suddenly Matt shook his head and waved his hands in the air in front of him, "No!" he blurted out. "Bullshit! This stuff doesn't happen. It can't happen! Oh, man!!"

Hank reached out and put his arm around Matt's shoulders. "It just did happen, buddy." He squeezed Matt's shoulder. "Please, don't get pissed, Matt. It's okay, I mean it. Nothing's gonna happen to ya, I swear." Hank's finger went back up to his mouth.

Matt looked over at George, his boss, who'd finally finished laughing some. George was still all smiles as he looked at Matt. Matt pointed his finger at his boss. "Are you really gay?" he asked incredulously. "Are you...really?"

"Oh, hell, Matt," George bellowed out still with a big smile. "I'm as gay as the day's long. Always have been. Me and Hank've been fuckin' each other since we were in high school. Here, I'll show ya," and he suddenly leaned over.

Before Matt could do anything, he felt his soft cock being sucked up into his boss's mouth. Matt gasped at the feel of his boss's tongue running all over his cock. At the same time, George reached over and grabbed hold of Hank's cock. Matt just looked wide-eyed at Hank. George let go of Matt's cock and moved over to suck Hank's cock some. Now, finally, Hank saw the beginnings of a smile sneaking into the corners of Matt's mouth. George let go of Hank's cock and looked back at Matt. "See?" he said to Matt and kept on smiling.

Matt's smile was full now and he let his head fall back. "Awww FUCK!" was all he could think to say. Now all three of them laughed. Matt looked at Hank, who still had his finger up to his mouth. "So you told him, didn't ya? You told him you were fucking me?"

Hank looked sheepish, but told Matt that, yes, he did tell George that they were fucking. "You see, Matt," Hank told him. "George here has the best gaydar on the planet. Every time he interviews for an opening in the store, he only hires guys he thinks are probably gay. My job is to lure you guys out here to my van to find out for sure."

Matt sat up now, his eyes widening and his mouth opening wider and wider. "NO!" he laughed. He put his hands up to his forehead, trying to digest what he was hearing. Then he looked at his boss. "So you knew? How the fuck did you know? I never told anybody!"

George laughed his booming laugh again. He was sitting cross-legged now facing the two of them. He reached out and tweaked Matt's dick. "I don't know how I know, buddy. I just know, that's all. I've always been able to tell who was gay and who wasn't. That's how I started fucking around with Hank back when we were in high school."

"So, you two've been fuckin' all the boys in the store?" Matt asked. He was still looking back and forth at the two men and down to the floor, trying to take it all in.

"Almost all of 'em!" George snickered. "Sometimes we all meet at Hank's house and have us one hell of an orgy. Now that you know, you're gonna have ta come join us."

Matt's face perked up at that one. His smile was all the answer the guys needed. They knew they now had one more.

"Wow!" was all Matt could think to say. "Fuckin' WOW!" he shook his head back and forth. "And I thought this kind of stuff only happened, like, in stories, or movies, or somethin'. Never thought it'd fuckin' happen to me!" He looked at George and sighed. "No wonder Corey wasn't worried about coming on to me in the break room! He already knew why I was hired!"

Suddenly Matt's eyes widened yet again. "HEY!" he yelled. He turned and pointed his finger at Hank. Hank's finger pressed against the corner of his lips and he squinted his eyes almost shut. "You already been fuckin' Corey, haven't ya? You been fuckin' him all this time, right?"

Hank moved his finger just a centimeter from his lips and said in a tiny, almost fearful voice, "Just a little bit."

The anger and disappointment Hank feared didn't come. Matt almost collapsed laughing. He rolled over and lay on top of Hank. Hank wrapped his arms around Matt and hugged him. He put both hands on Matt's face and raised his head up to face Hank. "Hey, buddy. I didn't know you would hook up with anyone else in the store. Not this fast, anyway. Listen - Corey is hands off if you say so. I mean it."

Matt just smiled and hugged Hank tighter. "Don't worry about it, Hank. If it weren't for you and George, Corey and me might not have met. You fuck me – you fuck him too if ya want." He grinned his sexy smile he learned always turned Hank on. "You can fuck both of us together if you want." He ground his cock into Hank's as he talked.

Hank was in complete agreement. He answered Matt with a quick kiss. Then Matt turned his newfound skills for charm onto George. He was still on top of Hank and turned his head to look at George. He reached back with both hands and spread his butt cheeks to show George his hole.

"So, boss," he smiled at George and wiggled his little butt. "I guess I don't have to worry about being fired, huh?" His charm worked.

"Hell no, I ain't gonna fire ya, Matt!" George boomed as he unzipped his pants. "I'm gonna fuck ya!"

■

DOUBLE COUPON DAY
– PART 2 –

REDEMPTION TIME

George arrived at the store to start work, and immediately headed for the back where the storerooms and the loading dock was. Today was a big day of the week for deliveries. He hated having three big semis show up on the same day, but he didn't control that part of the schedule. All he could do was try to schedule extra guys to work that day to get the trucks offloaded, and the stock put away as quickly as possible. He had to work the boys harder that day, but tried to make up for it by letting them take longer breaks and giving them an allowance for lunch so they could eat a good meal.

George was a good manager. Sure he liked fucking all those young butts, but he also liked taking care of his staff. He long ago started a fund that was approved by his store's chain to provide college scholarships for the top performers. It cost a little money in the beginning, but it also meant the top performers kept working at the store while they went to college, which in turn kept recruiting and training costs to a minimum, and made up for the cost of the scholarships. He knew for some time that teenagers and young college guys were getting into trouble because there were so few activities for them to do. So George got together with managers of other stores, and they organized several sports teams to give the guys something constructive and fun to do with some of their spare time. The stores all played against each other, but George couldn't let on that his store's team was a gay team.

The sports world is still not a place to be openly gay, especially for young guys. The straight players were too scared of losing a game to a gay team, and George knew they would get around it by refusing to play a gay team based on one fictitious conviction or another: whatever would mean the straight teams didn't have to play, that's what they would say.

Of course, there was another reason George liked to take care of his crew. He loved the way they dropped their pants and showed their appreciation! George always smiled thinking about the day he got an award from the home office for having the store with the lowest turnover rate. Many other managers asked him how he did it. He had to come up with any reason other than the real one!

The appreciation was another thing on George's mind while he walked into the back of the store. The guys were there all right, working hard to offload two trucks and make sure the perishable items got into the refrigerators and freezers quickly. The guys actually in the back of the trucks worked with their shirts off in the sunlight, something that was against the rules. But George knew the guys who wrote those rules never offloaded a truck in their lives, and figured what the hell? Let the guys work comfortable, give 'em a soda and a snack on their break, and they'd be happy. It worked.

George walked around the back, greeting the guys, clapping them on the back, playfully slapping a few butts, and whispering in an ear here and there. He stood and looked around, feeling that someone was missing.

"Hey, guys!" he yelled at them all. "Where's Corey?"

The other guys stopped working and looked at each other. It was clear to George that each one of them was waiting for someone else to say something. Some of them even looked guilty. That told George all he needed to know.

"God dammit!" he almost spat and headed out to the front of the trucks.

The other guys sighed and went back to work, but kept their eyes on George's back as he walked outside. George snuck up to the cab of the truck and listened. He heard what he was listening for and quietly stepped up to the driver's side window so he could look inside the cab. It was a cab with the sleeper in back, and George could just barely see into the back. Then he wrenched the door open, jumped inside, reached out and yanked the curtain open. There he saw Corey's blonde butt just as the driver pulled his cock out of it, dripping cum and spit.

"Dammit, Bill!" George yelled to the driver. "How many times I gotta tell ya not to fuck these boys at least 'til they're done emptyin' your rig?" Corey scrambled to pull his pants up. George wasn't pissed at Corey. Hell, these boys were young, healthy and horny, and he couldn't blame them just for that. But, the drivers should know better.

George gestured at Corey, "Get your damn pants up and get back to work!" he growled. His voice was rough but his eyes twinkled and Corey knew it. He snapped up his jeans and on the way out of the truck, he quickly reached out and gave his boss's crotch a quick squeeze. George reached out and grabbed Corey's arm, leaned over and whispered into Corey's ear. Corey flashed a smile and nodded quickly as he scrambled out of the truck. George and Bill heard the other guys laugh as Corey walked around the back of the truck.

"Damn, Corey!" they heard one laugh, "You're sweatin' more 'n me, dude!" There was laughter as they heard Corey hoot a couple of times. George turned to Bill, who still had his pants down as his cock softened.

"Jeez, Bill!" George said. "I got another truck comin' soon, and I gotta get yours emptied out and outta here. Can't ya help me out sometimes and keep your dick in your pants for a little while?" Bill just laughed since George still had the twinkle in his eye.

"Aw shit, George," he said in his southern drawl. "What am ah supposed to do? You know these boys like trucker cock!" he said as he smiled and put a finger right up to George's nose. "Just like y'all do!" George tried to look mean but it didn't work. He just shook his head. "Not when I'm working, Bill, you know that. Now get dressed and go inside somewhere...somewhere where I can see ya!" George sounded mean, but just before he turned to leave the truck he leaned down and gave Bill a kiss on his wet cock.

After he slipped out of the cab, he leaned back in and whispered something to Bill. Bill gave him a thumbs-up and then pulled his pants up. George walked back through the storeroom, his scowl daring all the smiling faces to say something. No one did, so George just shook his head and went back into the store. He had to walk through the break room to get to his office. There he saw Matt stuffing a backpack into his locker. George checked the clock and saw that Matt was almost 45 minutes early. He stopped and looked at Matt.

"Why so early, Matt?"

"Had practice this morning," Matt said. "I'm hungry so I'm gonna get something to eat before I clock in."

George crossed his arms in front of his chest and leaned up against the wall, looking at Matt and rolling his eyes. "Some *thing*, or some *body*?" he asked Matt.

Matt snickered. "Thing, boss, thing!" he laughed. They were alone in the break room. "If it was some body," Matt continued, "it would be you, boss. No one but you." He made a show of looking at George's crotch and smacking his lips.

George sighed. "Why the hell do I bother?" he asked no one in particular.

"'Cause you like the fringe benefits!" Matt laughed.

George looked around quickly to make sure no one came in. "You doin' anything Saturday night, Matt?" he asked.

Matt flashed his so sexy smile, "Nuthin' I can't get out of."

"Can you be at Hank's house around 8 or so?"

The smile got bigger. And sexier. "You got it, boss!"

Matt walked past George to the microwave. Without looking back he patted his little butt and said, "At least you'll get it Saturday night!" He knew George would be looking. He was right.

"God dammit!" George said again, but snickered as he walked on into his office. He wanted to call Hank. He saw Hank in the store a couple of days ago in the new boy's checkout line, and was anxious to know how it went. He closed his door, sat at his desk, and picked up his phone. The rest of the workday he didn't see the boys whispering into each other's ears and snickering. Nor did he notice that, every time he walked into the break room, whatever boys were in there talking quickly shut up.

Hank reported to George that the new boy was a no go. Well, it happened sometimes. George's gaydar was good, but he never did bat 1000. Sometimes, though, they later found out the guy was gay after all, but wasn't into car sex…while he was at work…on a new job…when he was clocked in. And sometimes he either wasn't into older guys, or not into anonymous sex. Some of them eventually came around. Hank said that Saturday was just fine with him. He never did say having one of their parties was a bad idea. He gladly changed his plans to accommodate them.

The next day, George made the rounds of the boys again, whispering into their ears that Saturday was confirmed. He walked into the break room in time to overhear Corey tell Matt that he had three, and that Matt had two.

"Two and three of what, guys?" George asked, startling the two.

"Um...papers, boss!" Matt said quickly. "Corey has three papers to write this semester and I have two." George went on into his office. He didn't see Corey and Matt look at each other and didn't hear them say, "Whew!" He also didn't hear Corey tell Matt that the stud who works in the meat department had six.

As the day wore on the boys whispered into each other's ears. Some had two, some didn't have any, and some had three or more. One shift passed the word to the next shift and asked how many each of them had.

Turns out there was an awful lot.

—

Hank lived outside the city in the house he grew up in, and eventually inherited from his parents. It was a big one: Four bedrooms upstairs, a living room, den, dining room, and kitchen downstairs. Hank finished a portion of the basement, turning it into a soundproof media room. A porch wrapped around the entire house. Out back was an old brick barbeque his dad had built years ago, and a little further back was a small pond with a raft floating on it that Hank made a long time ago. Hank wasn't a farmer but his dad was. When Hank moved back in, he sold off parts of the land to neighboring farmers. The profits from the sale pretty much guaranteed that Hank only worked when he felt like it. The nearest neighbor was out of sight about a half mile away, which meant Hank could make as much noise as he wanted, and could run around outside naked any time, day or night.

The boys weren't due until later that evening, but George arrived just after noon. He brought several bags of groceries from the store, one full of condoms. He joked about how much food those boys could put away, and always made sure he brought more than enough. He helped Hank cook and get the place ready for the party. Another friend of theirs, named Dan, would arrive later. Dan was a distributor for a large brewery and always brought a keg. The only thing the boys had to bring was their butts.

As the sun went down, Hank and George had the place ready, and were sitting arm in arm on the old porch swing with their feet intertwined. It was an old swing, and had been hanging ever since Hank was a kid.

They joked about all the times when the folks had gone out, especially the summer before Hank and George started college, and they sucked each other's cocks on that swing.

One day they were naked and going at it when one of Hank's big German Shepherds trotted up on the porch with one of his toys in his mouth, ready to fetch. He walked right up to the boys, who were completely oblivious to anything other than each other's cocks in their mouths. The dog's head tilted, watching them, and his ears twitched listening to the sounds of sucking and slurping and licking. Finally, the dog decided he and his toy had been ignored long enough. He let the toy slip out of his mouth, and then let out a single but very sharp bark right in the boys' ears.

Hank and George jumped straight up in the air like scared cats. Anyone who's ever not been careful on an old porch swing will tell you what will happen, and sure enough, both boys went over the back of it and smacked their naked butts on the porch. The nearest neighbor was half a mile away, but on that particular day they probably heard young Hank let out a string of cussin' that would have made a sailor pull his cock out as he called that poor dog all kinds of names, none of which could be found in the Bible.

Hank and George laughed at the memories and talked and kissed. They held off doing more than kissing though, telling each other they had to save themselves for the boys later. Hank's driveway was a long one, and they could always hear or see a car coming in plenty of time to get some clothes on before the driver could tell what was going on. That's why they got away with so much when they were younger. As the sun vanished, they saw the first set of headlights appear in the distance.

It was Jess, a night shifter who worked stocking the store. He honked as he drove around the house to park in the back. Both the guys were surprised when Jess walked around front with two other guys who Hank and George didn't know.

"Hey boss! Hey Hank!" Jess called out as he walked up the stairs to the porch. The two guys with him just nodded and smiled a little sheepishly.

Jess pointed to them each in turn. "This is Tom, and that's Willy. They're buddies of mine. Hope it's okay to bring 'em?"

Hank and George smiled and nodded but glanced sharply at Jess, who laughed.

"Fuck buddies, guys – fuck buddies!" Jess told them. "They want to join us is all."

Now Hank's and George's smiles widened.

"Well, hell guys, nice to meet ya!" Hank shook their hands with George. "Come on in! The more the merrier, ya know?" Hank winked at Jess and ushered them all inside. He turned around and shrugged his shoulders at George and gave him a thumbs-up.

Even though Dan hadn't arrived with the keg yet, Jess had told Tom and Willy the rules.

Hank knew better than to expect the guys who weren't 21 yet to stay away from the beer. He only had one pair of eyes and they weren't in the back of his head. He also remembered how young he was when he and George started sneaking beers from their dad's supply. He knew it would be a waste of time to try to watch all the guys and fuck, too. So, anyone driving had to either come prepared to spend the night, or not come at all. The boys followed Hank into the den and dropped their car keys into an empty drawer in Hank's desk, which Hank promptly locked. Only he and George knew where he hid the key.

Bill arrived next in his jeans and boots, a bandana tied around his head, and a shirt with the sleeves cut off, showing off his trucker's tattoos. They were still in the den when they heard the doorbell ring. Corey stuck his head in the door and hollered out asking if anyone was home. Hank hollered back joking that they didn't have to ring the bell. Especially not Corey and Matt. They both lived in the dorms now and went to different colleges, so it was tough for them to meet up in each other's rooms. Hank had given both of them a key to his house, and they made a lot of use of one of his spare bedrooms, sometimes alone with each other, and sometimes dragging Hank into the room with them.

Corey and Matt came in hand-in-hand and met Hank in the hallway. They hugged and the boys noticed the strangers in the living room.

"Don't worry about it, guys," Hank told them. "They're friends of Jess's from his school. They came to join us."

"So it's cool if we bring someone with us, huh?" Matt asked.

"Hell yeah!" Hank grinned, and grabbed his package. "I'm ready if they are!"

"Man that's good to hear," Corey said as Hank turned to go in the living room. "'Cause we brought a few with us, too."

Hank froze. He turned just as Corey opened the front door and beckoned. Hank's eyes widened as five more guys walked into the hallway. Corey pointed them out to Hank.

"These are my buddies Ben, Justin, and Tim, and that's Matt's buds, JJ and Vince."

"Well, come on in, boys!" a flustered Hank told them. George was in the kitchen pulling trays of food from the oven and almost dropped one of them when he saw the extra guys walk by. Hank went in the kitchen and told George who they were while Corey dropped his keys into the desk drawer.

Dan was the next to arrive, and some of the boys helped him bring in the keg and the paraphernalia that went with it. They went to set it up on the back porch. George caught Matt's shirt collar as he walked by and playfully pulled Matt back to him. "Papers, eh?" he grinned at Matt. "You got two *papers* to write, eh?" Matt just gave George a quick kiss and giggled as he went out to the porch to get some beer.

Someone called out that Mikey had arrived. In the kitchen, George caught Corey coming back from the porch with a beer. He put his hands on his hips and scowled at Corey.

"And does Mikey have *papers* to write too?" Corey gave George a big shit-eating grin and danced just out of George's reach while rubbing his crotch.

"He sure does, boss," Corey laughed. "He's got about six of 'em!"

"*Shit*!!" George bellowed out. Hank joked that he hoped George brought enough food this time. "Oh, don't worry, guys," Corey told them. "We knew we'd throw a kink in things so we all chipped in. Mikey made up some deli trays to bring. We're fine." He went into the living room, leaving Hank and George to stand in the kitchen with their mouths open.

All told, there were about a dozen guys from the store. They almost all went to different schools and had found their own fuck buddies. They did some planning together, and tonight they all brought as many of their own buddies as could make it. Over the next hour, guys just kept streaming in the front door: Tall guys, short guys, buff guys and skinny guys: guys with long hair, short hair, spiked hair, and colored hair: guys with hairy bodies, smooth bodies, tattoos and piercings. The house was filling up quickly, and the crowd spilled over into the den, kitchen, and on the back porch. Shit, guys, I'm writing this damn thing and even I lost count of how many guys ended up in that house!

The four dads were all sitting in the living room – in some sort of shock – and were just looking at each other and smiling. The guys from the store were bringing beers to everyone and seeing to everyone, like they'd taken over that duty from Hank and George. Hank was wondering how he was going to get things started. Usually it was easy with the guys from the store since they'd done this so many times before. It had become something of a ritual, and getting everyone to get naked wasn't a problem at all, but now he was just sitting on the sofa, mesmerized at the parade of great looking guys walking in and out of the room.

Corey came into the living room, put a CD in Hank's stereo, and turned up the volume. It was a CD of techno music; the kind usually heard in bars for the go-go boys to dance to. And that was what Corey started to do. As the beat filled the air, he stood in the middle of the room facing Hank and the other dads, and did a little jig while eyeing them and licking his lips to tease them. Then, while they were watching him, he leaned over and grabbed Matt's hand. Matt stood, and now both of them were starting a dance to the music, and others started to cheer them on.

Someone yelled, "Take it off, dudes!" and Matt and Corey embraced each other and started dancing together. While the guys all watched, Matt put his arms around Corey's neck, and they kissed. "Yeah!!" several of the guys yelled, and Hank and George applauded and smiled. Matt turned around and leaned backwards into Corey. He raised his arms back up and around Corey's neck behind him. Corey was taller than Matt, and leaned his head down to kiss Matt again, with his arms and hands running up and down Matt's body, squeezing his pecs and stomach and groping his crotch. Matt raised his arms straight up in the air and Corey smoothly pulled Matt's T-shirt up and off, and tossed it behind him.

More applause, more shouted encouragement, as Corey used his hands to show off Matt's chest and belly button and reach down to cup a now very prominent bulge in Matt's jeans. The two ground their hips together in time with the music. Matt reached behind him and grabbed Corey's butt and let the other guys watch him squeeze the cheeks. Another turn, and they were facing each other and kissing again, still grinding their hips together, but hard and raunchy now, all with the other guys' full encouragement. Matt's hands slipped inside Corey's tank and pulled it off. It too, was simply tossed in the air. Corey leaned down and started licking and kissing Matt's chest. The guys all hooted and hollered and were now clapping in time with the beat, and more than a few were trying to clap and adjust their growing packages at the same time.

Corey worked his mouth down Matt's gyrating body and finally ended up on his knees with his tongue licking Matt's belly button. Matt's chest was shiny from Corey's tongue. Matt was bucking his hips in time to the music and pushing his bulge into Corey's face. Every time the beat sent Matt's crotch into Corey, Corey opened his mouth, and very soon a wet spot showed up on Matt's crotch. Corey looked at the dads and the other guys standing behind them, and smiled a wicked, lusty smile at them. Then he flicked his right hand around like a magician would to draw attention to it, reached over and smoothly pulled Matt's zipper down.

The guys hooted, hollered, applauded, and cheered the two of them on. Another magic move with his hand and Corey unsnapped Matt's jeans, which started to slide down over his hips. Matt gyrated his hips even harder and his jeans slid down his legs by themselves, revealing some black boxer briefs with white letters across his dick spelling out the words, "Home of the Whopper."

Just as the music reached a crescendo heading to the finish, Corey, still on his knees, reached down and held Matt's jeans to the floor. Matt didn't step out of them, but jumped out of them, high up in the air, came down, and landed rigid with his left arm up and his right hand in front of his obviously hard dick with his pelvis thrust way out. At the same time the music ended and Matt froze, Corey yanked the briefs down and Matt's cock popped up and waved to everyone.

The guys went wild. They applauded and hollered and hooted and yelled for more. Hank and the dads looked at each other and knew what each was thinking: 'Those little fuckers have been *rehearsing* this!'

Before any of them had time to say anything, another song started and Matt put his hand on Corey's forehead and pushed. Corey ended up lying on his back on the floor with his legs spread and Matt danced naked around him.

The guys were hollering and clapping so loud someone had to reach over and turn the volume up on the stereo. Corey was lying with his feet almost touching the dads sitting on the sofa. Matt straddled Corey, facing his feet, and spent a few seconds bucking his hips and making his dick bounce up and down. He kept dancing and started squatting down slowly, slowly, and slowly, with the applause and whistling and hollering building until his butt finally came to rest on Corey's face, and everyone let out one big, loud, "YEAH!!" Hank and the dads just stared with their mouths hanging open. They were all thinking that they wouldn't see anything this good in any bar in their city!

Matt kept his butt on Corey's face and while still on his knees he leaned way back, resting on his hands behind him with his cock sticking up in the air. Corey reached around and stroked Matt's meat in time with the music. Matt let his head fall back and enjoyed it for a few seconds, then had to straighten up and push Corey's hand away so he didn't cum too soon. Matt made a show of leaning forward and reached just inside the waistband of Corey's jeans. He pulled a ring out, and the guys saw that it was a key chain ring with about three inches of chain that was attached to Corey's zipper. Matt raised his wet butt up off Corey's face, and stood up while Corey stayed on the floor. Matt used his foot and toes to squeeze Corey's pecs and play with his chest. Matt worked his foot down Corey's body and the guys watched as Matt stuck his big toe inside the ring of the key chain. The music reached a point where it suddenly stopped for a couple of seconds, and in the quick silence the guys heard as Matt used his toe in the ring to pull Corey's zipper down. Then the music started back up again but was almost drowned out by the applause.

Corey had his hands behind his head, like he was relaxing, and still gave the dads in front of him a sexy smile. Corey knew he and Matt had them, and had them good. Corey raised his feet up off the floor and put one in Hank's lap and the other in George's. The guys knew what to do and they both grabbed a cuff and together they pulled Corey's pants off and tossed them behind them. Corey had on the same kind of black boxer briefs that Matt had on, but no lettering on the front. Matt was still dancing around Corey, now and then using his feet to tease. He'd use his toes to play with Corey's crotch or would stick them in Corey's mouth for him to quickly suck.

Then Matt put his foot on Corey's side and pretended to push and Corey rolled over onto his stomach. Across the butt of his underwear in white letters were the words, "Home *for* the Whopper."

Matt was still dancing over Corey, and Corey was squirming on the floor and humping his butt up and down in time to the music. Matt pointed a finger to Bill and then pointed to Corey's butt. Bill didn't need to be told twice and he leaned over, reached out, and pulled Corey's briefs off and tossed them behind him. Now both boys were naked and Matt again used his foot on Corey's side and Corey rolled over again showing the guys his hard dick. The applause was thunderous.

Matt once again straddled Corey's face and reached out, grabbed Corey's dick, and held it straight up. Corey reached up, grabbed Matt's dick, and pointed it at his own face. Once again, just as the song reached its loud finish, both Matt and Corey jammed each other's dicks in their mouths. The guys went wild and it seemed the whole house shook.

The boys jumped up and took their bows; then Matt went to the sofa next to Hank. He gave Hank his typical sexy boyish smile and said, "Surprise!!"

"What the hell...?" was all Hank could think to say. Corey went and sat on George's lap facing him. Jess walked up to Dan, and Mickey from the meat department stood in front of Bill while both boys unzipped their pants.

"You haven't figured it out yet?" Matt laughed at Hank.

"What?" Hank looked like he was almost hypnotized.

"You guys have been taking good care of us boys," Matt said as he put one knee up on the sofa and halfway straddled Hank's lap. He put a hand up and stroked Hank's face, "giving us a place to fuck," he stuck a finger in Hank's mouth and his other hand reached out to Hank's crotch, "and a reason to fuck!"

Corey continued, "We know when you guys were young as us you bent over and gave your butts to some other guys all the time, right?" The dads just nodded.

"Well," Jess said, "tonight you're gonna do it again!"

The dads' eyes widened even more.

"That's right, guys," Mickey teased as he and Jess pulled their hard cocks out, "we're turnin' the tables on ya. Tonight every damn one of us is gonna fuck you silly!"

Hank opened his mouth to say something, but Matt quickly threw his other leg up over the back of the sofa and slid his dick into Hank's mouth. The other boys did the same and the dads suddenly had some young meat stuffed in their mouths. Hank forgot all about whatever the hell it was he was going to say, and just sucked instead.

Well, that started it. The dads opened their eyes, but all they could see in front of them was a bush of hair. They didn't see the air suddenly filled with shirts and socks and jeans and shorts and underwear, as the whole crowd got naked all at once. They didn't see the crowd of guys spread back into the other rooms and go to it. It was obvious to them now that all these guys had spent some time orchestrating the whole night, and in silent agreement they just went with it.

Matt and the boys kept right on fucking the dads' faces, and while the dads couldn't see, they felt other hands on their bodies pulling their clothes off. They felt a mouth belonging to somebody clamp down on their cocks and start sucking. Hands pushed and pulled and all four dads wound up with their legs spread wide and their feet up and a tongue started licking their fuck holes. Each dad had three boys working on him and they loved it. And, there was plenty more where that came from.

By some agreement obviously reached earlier, the boys from the store who already knew the dads got the first shot. Matt pulled his dick out of Hank's mouth – somewhat reluctantly – and whoever was eating Hank's ass moved up to continue Hank's face fucking. Matt got between Hank's legs, held them apart, and with a hoot, slid his dick up that chute and started fucking hard. Hank managed to let out a moan but didn't try to say anything. Besides, it's rude to talk with your mouth full.

The other dads let out similar noises as their holes got plugged full with young dick. They all heard a voice from somewhere holler out, "All right!! They's gettin' fucked!!" With all their holes stuffed full and their cocks getting sucked there was no way for the dads to communicate with each other but, like all long time buddies, they didn't need to. They just enjoyed.

Matt was the first, and threw his head back, sucked in a breath, gritted his teeth, and jack hammered ole Hank's ass while he filled it full of twink cum. As hot as he got dancing with Corey for the guys, he just couldn't hold back. Turns out neither could the other boys. All four dads got their butts slicked up with cum almost at the same time.

The dads didn't know how they did it, but somehow, with all the other fucking going on, the boys kept some kind of watch. Soon as Matt and the others pulled out of the guys' butts, there were four fresh boys ready with their dicks in their hands. The guys fucking face pulled out and the dads only had a couple of seconds while the boys changed places.

They all opened their eyes, and all they saw in the room was naked flesh. Then their mouths got stuffed by fresh cock, and some of the boys moved down and took over fucking their butts. Matt, Corey, Jess, and Mickey could be heard all through the house hollering and high-fiving each other on their way to the back porch for more beer. The other guys just went right on fucking. The dads got another load of cum shot up their butts and the boys changed places again. This time the dads used their couple of seconds without a dick in their mouths to glance at each other. Although they all had huge smiles on their faces, the same thought could be read in their eyes, 'Can we take *all* these guys?' Then they were sucking again and a fresh dick slid up their butts.

The guys who knew each other fucked bareback, and the guys who didn't know anyone else used a condom. Hank was thinking that he would always joke with George about bringing a whole sack full of condoms each time…joke's over now! Now Hank was wondering if George had brought enough!

The sounds of fucking were all over the house now. There was sighing and slurping and squishing and moaning, and the temperature in the place was steadily climbing. All through the house, anytime someone opened his mouth someone else stuck a dick in it. Anytime someone's butt came into view someone else stuck a dick or a face in it. Guys who'd never topped before were topping now, and guys who'd never bottomed before were grunting and taking it. If a guy stood up he suddenly got his dick sucked and his ass eaten.

If anyone had looked through Hank's living room window from the outside, they wouldn't have been able to tell if the floor was carpeted or not. It was covered with bodies. Naked bodies. Sweaty bodies. Undulating bodies that were between a pair of legs with feet up in the air all through the room. Butts were humping up and down and heads were bobbing up and down and now and then a squirt of cum would fly through the air.

One bottom guy was spread out in a chair and a top guy was fucking his ass while standing up. He was fucking and jacking the guy at the same time. The guy in the chair came, and when he shot, his cum flew up in the air like a popcorn kernel, and the top caught it in his mouth. He managed to catch each squirt and kept right on fucking at the same time. That earned some admiration from whoever saw it, and then others were trying it, too.

Soon the sounds of fucking were mixed with the smell of fucking as cum was shooting everywhere. The boys – being boys – never stopped, and certainly weren't "done" just because they'd already shot a load or four. George wondered how much cum there would be if they managed to save all of it. But then, a guy sometimes thinks weird stuff when he's getting royally gangbanged.

After a while Hank and George decided to take a break. Not because they didn't like however many dicks they'd had up their butts so far, but because their legs were getting cramped from being in the same position for so long: spread. They walked through the living room and tried not to step on anyone on the floor and headed for the kitchen. A couple of the boys went with them and stuck with them. George mentioned that he wanted a beer and one of the boys ran and got one for him and Hank. They walked out to the back porch to take a piss but found out there was no room. There were naked bodies fucking and sucking out there, too. They walked on out in the back yard and saw that some of the guys were skinny-dipping in the pond and some were fucking on the bank. There were even a couple of guys in the middle of the pond in a 69 on the old raft.

The boys stuck right with Hank and George. They sat down in the grass and the boys sat down with them. That was when Hank and George realized they were being "attended." Hank mentioned that he was hungry and one of the boys got up and ran into the house to make him a sandwich. Hank looked at the other guy, whom he didn't even know.

"Are you 'assigned' to us?" Hank smiled to him.

"Sure," the boy said and leaned into Hank. "You like?"

"Hell, I could get used to this!" Hank laughed and wrapped his arm around the boy. He let his hand slide down to the boy's dick and the boy spread his legs automatically and let Hank stroke him. "Yeah," Hank whispered, "I could get *real* used to this!" The boy tilted his head up and Hank kissed him.

"How long have you guys been planning this?" George asked.

"Well," the boy answered, "Jess talked to me a bit about three months ago I guess."

Hank and George just looked at each other.

George stretched out and started eating the boy's butt while Hank jacked him off. When the other boy came back outside with Hank's sandwich he found his buddy's legs spread out and his buddy was moaning. Hank managed to eat his sandwich and jack the boy off at the same time. The other boy used his tongue like a napkin to lick the mayonnaise off the corners of Hank's lips and chin while he ate.

Soon they were both laying back and making out. Neither Hank nor George could help themselves. These boys were just too beautiful, and the whole scene was just too hot. They climbed on top of the boys and fucked them on the grass. While they were still sweating the boys rolled them over and returned the favor. Hank and George walked with the boys back to the light of the porch with cum dripping off their smiling faces.

There on the porch they saw Bill and Dan with their arms wrapped around a boy each, and they were all making out. One of the boys had one leg raised and wrapped around Bill's tattooed butt and Bill had the boy pushed up against the wall. Hank knew that if he came outside a couple of minutes later the boy would have both legs wrapped around Bill, and Bill would be fucking him right up against the wall. He was right.

In the kitchen, Hank told the boy who was with him to stay right there for a minute, he wanted to check something. He left the boy sipping a beer and tiptoed upstairs. He snuck down the hall and peeked around the door to one of the spare bedrooms. Sure enough, Matt and Corey were on the bed, their bodies pressed close together. They were making out and their hands and legs were slowly, sensually, sliding over each other. That's why Hank didn't see them after they all started fucking. Hank just smiled and tiptoed back downstairs.

In the kitchen he found a different boy sipping a beer and waiting for him. He asked where the other guy was. The new boy put his arms around Hank and pulled him close and kissed him. "He already had his turn up your ass outside," the boy whispered in Hank's ear. "Now I want mine!" and Hank wound up getting his ass fucked as he bent over the kitchen counter. George was on the floor on his stomach and he also had a new boy humping away on his ass. And the fucking went on and on.

It was early fall, and while the outside temperatures weren't quite hot enough to turn on the air conditioner, the inside was heating up! More and more of the boys spilled outside to fuck on the porch, or on the grass, or out by the pond. The bodies coming out the kitchen door were sweatier and sweatier, so Hank managed to crawl out from under the boys who were fucking him long enough to turn on the back yard's sprinklers. Now everyone was fucking and sucking and getting rinsed off at the same time. Hank wished he'd thought to set up a video camera. The cool water seemed to wake the guys up some and the action outside got more enthusiastic. The boys dragged the dads outside and out into the grass under the sprinklers and the dads kept right on getting pounded by dick after dick after dick.

Finally Hank saw Mickey lay down next to him. "You mean it's your turn again?" Hank asked him and laughed.

Mickey laughed right back, "Yeah! You want us all again?" he rolled on top of Hank and kissed him.

"Yes, but not tonight!" Hank laughed and ran his fingers through Mickey's hair. "I used to only worry about having a hangover when I woke up," he said. "Now I'll worry if my ass is ever gonna close up!"

"Don't worry, Hank," Mickey told him between kisses. "You're as tight as you ever were, and you always will be."

Hank and Mickey went back into the kitchen to get something to eat. Fucking all night works up an appetite. The food was going over very well, but there was still plenty left. There were some other boys there munching on sandwiches and meatballs and buffalo wings. They all smiled at Hank and asked him if he liked the evening.

"Hell, yes, boys!!" Hank laughed. He grabbed his cock and held it up for the boys to see. "Even my piss slit is curved into a smile!"

George came in with Jess, and then Dan came in with another boy from the store, and it was evident that between the four dads, they'd taken all those young dicks up their butts and apparently were going to live to tell about it.

Around the island counter in the kitchen, the dads finally got the boys to talk. They'd been planning this for months. It started when Jess went to see Mickey at his dorm and one of Mickey's fuck buddies was there. They had a little fun making out and groping each other, but had to stop when Mickey's straight roommate showed up with a buddy, a couple of girls, and some beer. Outside the room, Jess mentioned, "what if?" and that started things. A few of the other boys were old enough and worked as dancers and strippers in a couple of gay bars in town, and they were the ones who taught Matt and Corey the dance moves and timing, and they'd been practicing for the past two months just to do that one dance. The dads were impressed!

Dan and Bill came in the kitchen and said they'd found a few of the guys had fallen asleep outside. That's when Hank's head snapped up and he asked where the hell were they gonna put all those guys up? Jess just smiled and the dads figured they had a plan for that, too.

"We all brought sleeping bags and stuff, Hank. Don't worry, we thought of stuff ourselves."

Out of the car trunks came bags and pillows. Some of the guys used the showers in the house but most of them just jumped in the pond and washed up there. Some of the boys slept in the house and some stayed outside, but all of them had a place to sleep, and all of them had a pillow, and none of them slept alone.

Hank went upstairs toward his room, but first went further down the hall. His suspicions were correct, and he got a blanket from the closet and covered Matt and Corey, who were already asleep with their arms wrapped around each other. Hank tiptoed back down the hallway. In another room Dan and Bill had a couple of the boys between them in the king sized bed there. Hank gave them a thumbs-up. The next room was George's and while the blankets covered things it was obvious he had company, too.

Hank went on in his room and found two of the boys he didn't know already in his bed with some space left between them. They were smiling at him. One of them tossed back the covers and patted the empty mattress between them.

"Come on," he grinned at Hank. "We been waitin' for ya."

Hank laughed and shook his head. "Looks real good, boys!" he told them and sighed. "But us old farts can only last so long and then we need our rest. I've reached that point, I think." He lay down between them. It took about an hour and some more sweat, but the boys proved him wrong. They all fell asleep with Hank's hand cupping one of the boy's butts and his other hand holding on to the other's soft cock.

—

They had fallen asleep just as the sun was coming up, and Hank woke up in the middle of the afternoon. He was on his stomach. He smiled as he oriented himself. The boys were still sleeping on either side of him, and their legs were tangled with each other's. Hank didn't even try to remember how many cocks he'd taken up his ass last night, but he could still feel one in there. Or two. He reached back and felt his ass, and was surprised that it felt slippery! He sat up and reached out to the sleeping boys and felt their dicks. One was dry and the other was as slippery as his own ass was. Hank's smile got bigger. 'Damn!' he thought. 'That little squirt just got done fucking me again! That's why I woke up!' The boy just moaned a bit and turned over but didn't wake up. The smell of coffee was wafting up from the kitchen.

Hank managed to get out of bed without waking the boys up and went downstairs. Some of the boys were already awake, but most were still sleeping crammed into their sleeping bags in the house and outside. A few boys were gathered naked around the island counter in the kitchen, sipping coffee. Hank greeted them and got his own cup.

"I'll get some breakfast goin' soon as some more guys wake up," he told the boys.

"No, no!" the boys smiled and one said. "We'll take care of it, Hank." He leaned into Hank for a quick kiss. "All part of the service!"

Hank shook his head and smiled. "Be careful boys, or I'll get awful used to this," he warned them.

They sat and drank coffee and talked about their schools and the set up Hank and George had. Hank told them how it had actually started as soon as George transferred to the store. Hank had a young fuck buddy whose summer job ended just as school started in the fall. George had just started at the store and Hank fixed it with George so his buddy could work at the store. George even fixed the boy's work schedule to fit around his classes. Hank stopped in to visit George one day soon after, and George pointed to one of the boys pushing a line of grocery carts into the store.

"He's gay for sure," George told Hank.

"Damn cute, too!" Hank said. Hank told his buddy about the guy and his buddy got the guy alone one evening and came on to him. It worked. In the beginning, Hank's buddy did all the seducing, and George just naturally hired the guys he was sure was gay. Same thing he did at his other store; except he didn't have Hank around to help him out. George never came on to the guys himself: he had to think about sexual harassment suits.

It didn't take long before Hank was busy out in the back of his van. Some of the guys went for it and some didn't. Although nothing overt went on, it just seemed the guys who didn't go for it moved on to other jobs quickly, and soon the store had a good crowd of horny young guys to play around with. The orgies at Hank's house naturally followed, and apparently were becoming legendary.

Hank told the boys in the kitchen, "And you guys come on over any ole time we get together!" He was assured that he wouldn't have a problem with attendance at all.

Other boys were waking up, both inside and outside, and as guys usually do, they woke up horny. Anyone could glance around and see sleeping bags getting twisted up and thrown off as the guys went through a quick wake up fuck before they wandered into the kitchen.

Hank took out his biggest fry pans and a few of the guys took over, and even though it was officially dinnertime, they cooked up a feast of eggs and sausage and bacon and ham and hash browns and biscuits and toast. Hank went back upstairs to wake up the boys who had slept with him.

They were already half awake and pulled Hank back down between them, and with their morning hard-ons they went to work on Hank while breakfast was being prepared. Hank found himself the meat in a fuck sandwich as he plowed one guy's butt while getting rammed by the other guy. While they licked cum off each other Hank said once again how he could get used to this.

After breakfast, the boys went to work cleaning up the place. The dads only had to sit back and drink their coffee, watch, and smile. The house was full of naked boys flitting back and forth. One of them got a garden rake from the garage and was using it in the living room to rake up all the used condoms and wrappers and Kleenex. Clean-up didn't take long at all with so many boys at it.

Some of them had to go to work here and there, and some had to get back to their dorm rooms, hole up and study for some Monday exams. Since it was a weekend, George wasn't working but some of the boys had to go to the store. Their clothes had become one big pile in the den and they all had to spend some time searching through it to find their own stuff, and retrieve their keys from the desk drawer. One by one the boys came out of the den wearing wrinkled shirts and shorts and jeans. They all laughed and no one cared.

They all gave the dads' cocks one last kiss before they headed out the door.

Hank and George wound up right back on the old porch swing, naked, with their arms around each other, and their feet intertwined. Hank mentioned that next time they should set up some video cameras around the house since it seemed the population of their parties had suddenly grown.

"When we're too old to get it up anymore we'll at least have some memories to watch in the old fags' home," he laughed at George.

They heard a noise in the house and went inside to see what it was. At first it seemed nothing was wrong. Then they heard footsteps on the stairs and realized they had completely forgotten about them when a naked and smiling Corey and Matt came downstairs fresh from the shower. Since they fell asleep before anyone else, they also woke up first while the rest of the place was still asleep. Rather than wake everyone else up, they stayed in bed. Where the others fucked, they made love, slowly and sensually exploring each other's bodies, using their lips, tongues, fingertips and toes, and each concentrated on what the other liked. The blanket Hank had put over them ended up on the floor. They didn't talk, but just enjoyed the feeling of each other. Though it was slow and quiet, it was also beautiful and special. They took a long time at it and the end result was just as intense as anything else that had happened through the night. Newly exhausted, they'd slept through the whole afternoon while the other boys ate and cleaned up.

They fixed themselves something to eat, and then joined Hank and George on the porch. They sat on the porch at Hank and George's feet while they ate. Since neither of them had anything much going on at school, Hank told them to go ahead and spend the rest of the weekend at his house. They could go out and rent some movies and get some steaks to put out on the grill. Corey climbed up into Hank's lap and Matt sat in George's. They had to be really careful, or else they'd fall over the back of the swing and smack their naked butts on the porch.

■

ROBBY'S FIRST WAS A DOUBLE

Everyone has a "first time" story but not everyone tells theirs. Think I'll switch from one group to the other and tell you guys mine. See, I was lucky. My first time was cool. No quick fucks in a bathroom stall for *me*! Oh, no. And you'd never see *me* sprawled over a trashcan in an alley somewhere. No way. Not me. *I'm* sophisticated. *I'm* classy. *My* first time was intricately planned, and flawlessly executed.

Not by me – by the guy who nailed me. I was fuckin' clueless.

Took me a long time to finally be able to stand up and say it out loud and in front of people, but I was an abused child. I was the youngest in a family that included some "step" relatives. I was always the one blamed, framed, and maimed. And I do mean maimed. I got the hickory switch (that I was required to select myself. If it wasn't good enough I was whipped for that). Also got the belt a lot, too. Against my bare ass. I've been thrown across the room and slammed up against walls, then slapped open palm and backhand. Had pots, pans, spoons, eggs, and other food thrown at me. Seems my butt was always marked in one way or another. Either with bruises, welts, or scabs where I'd bled. My older brother used to practice his boxing skills on me. That was okay with everybody. It only became an issue when I tried to fight back; especially if I dared to leave a mark on him. He used to hide around corners, wait for me to come by, and beat the shit out of me. If I told my dad I got beat for being a tattler.

My dad caught me one day with drugs in my pocket. Pot and speed (I don't do drugs anymore). I was grounded my entire senior year in high school.

Not that any one at school noticed. The shit didn't stop with my family. The whole fucking town got into it: typical for small town America. Thinking back, I know that I always knew I was gay. It definitely wasn't something safe to talk about in my little town, but even though I denied it to myself, everyone else knew. In high school I was known as the "Freshman Faggot," the "Homeroom Homo." I would get hate notes shoved into the little slits in my locker addressed to the "Klass Kweer." The only time I had any friends or anyone to socialize with was when I had drugs to share. When my pockets were empty, so were the streets.

Sorry guys. Didn't mean that to be such a downer, but maybe now you can understand why, on the day I turned 18, I left. Spent the day going around to my relatives collecting my birthday money, and at 2:00 am after everyone else had gone to sleep, I left. Picked up the grocery bag full of my jeans and extra t-shirts I'd hid earlier in the garage and just walked away. Walked down the quarter mile country driveway, down the road 'til it curved out of sight of my house, and to this day I have yet to look back.

I went to Papa C's place. Papa C was an old Greek guy who ran an all night restaurant/bar at the edge of town. He was from old Greece. His last name had two hundred some odd letters in it, but it started with C. He looked like everybody's grandpa. Overweight, bald head except for the sides, and that was all gray. His place was a bar until 2:00 AM. After that all the kids my age would come in for soda and non-alcoholic drinks until 6:00 AM. There were lots of bars in town, but Papa C had the only place other than the few burger joints where underage kids like me could gather. Papa C was a loveable old guy who treated all us kids like his own grandkids. We would talk to him about things we were too scared to talk to our own folks about. I always knew I was welcome at Papa C's place, even if it was only by Papa C himself.

I got there that night about 3:00 am, got a soda and sat down at a table. I was wondering how I was going handle the confrontation with my folks that I knew would come soon as they figured out I wasn't coming home. Papa C came over and sat down with me. He gave me his famous critical eye (with a wink).

"You look like shit," he told me.

"Gee, thanks," I said, then lowered my eyes. "But yeah, I feel like shit." He just nodded. One thing about Papa C all the kids liked. He always listened. You'd always see him walking through his place when the kids were there, usually with his arm around somebody, dispensing advice without lecturing. Talking to us, but not talking down to us. Yeah, we all liked Papa C.

And then I, like a lot of kids before me, said, "Hey, Papa C." I looked around to make sure no one could hear me, (again, like a lot of kids before me), "Can I talk to you?"

"Shoot," he said. Well, that started it. Spilled my guts. Talked 'til the place closed at 6. Papa C led me to a back room, with his arm around my shoulder when I couldn't hold back the tears.

"Listen," he told me. "You just took a big step; took a lot out of you. What you gonna do next – you worry about later. There's a room upstairs with a bed in it. Go get some sleep. As far as I know I ain't seen you all week. Go get some rest. We figure something out when you wake up."

I stayed at Papa C's place two nights. On the third night I was sitting at a table about 3:00 am when Sanka came in. Sanka, of course, isn't his real name, but I like the movie, "Cool Runnings," so I'll call him Sanka. He was from Jamaica or French Polynesia or somewhere down there. He was black as coal and spoke with the coolest accent. I'd seen him several times in Papa C's and talked to him, but didn't really know him all that well, and never saw him any where other than Papa C's. Word was that he was gay, but he wasn't the outcast that I was. He was in college but no one knew just how old he was (I found out later he was 36). He was a witty guy and always made all of us laugh, so he was kind of accepted by everyone.

Sanka got a cup of coffee ("Java" he called it) and sat at my table.

"You look like shit, mon," he told me with no preamble, just the way Papa C said it. I replied the same way I did with Papa C. "Heard you left your folks. Stayin' here?" he asked me.

"Yeah."

"What you goin' to do? Where you goin' to go, mon?"

"Dunno. I'll find somethin'."

"No need to look so bad, mon," he said. "Come stay at my place. I have a small house, but just me, and no one to talk to. I could use some company. Come on."

I grabbed my grocery bag, thanked Papa C, and went to Sanka's house. Sanka gave me the grand tour, which took all of two and a half minutes. A tiny living room. A kitchen/dining combo, one bedroom. Sanka pointed to his bed. "That's it, mon. That's where we sleep." And a tiny bathroom.

Back in the living room, beer in hand, joint in his mouth, Sanka said, "Don' worry, mon. You okay here. No one to bother you. What you want, mon? Something to eat? More beer? Here – have another hit," and passed me the joint. Joint? More like a cigar. Sanka said that's the way they roll them down where he was from. I thought of the bathroom sink I'd used the past three days to wash up in, and told him I could really use a good shower.

"No problem, mon. Take your time. You know something? You too tense! After you shower, I will give you de best massage you will ever have your whole life. You will feel good."

The beer and pot was taking hold. "Sounds good to me!" I said. I went into the bathroom, stripped, and stood under the shower for a long time. Then it finally connected that when Sanka showed me the bedroom, he told me it's where "we" sleep. *'Oh my God!'* I thought, *'He wants to fuck me!'* Then I thought about it some more. *'Allright! I'm gonna do it! I'm fucking gonna do it!'*

I came out of the bathroom with a towel wrapped around my waist. Sanka had a couple of candles burning and passed me another joint (he must have finished the other one by himself!). I took a big hit and sat it in an ash tray. It wasn't the same stuff he gave me earlier. This was much better. Exploded in my head. "Wow!" I said. "What the hell is *that?*"

"Columbian, mon," he answered. "Best in all de world! You feeling good now, eh?"

"You got *that* right!"

Sanka told me to lay on the bed on my stomach, which I did. "No, no, mon," he said, "You got to be relaxed," and he worked the towel away from me. *'Yeah!'* I thought. I was nervous, but felt strangely sexy laying naked on his bed. *'Fuckin' A,'* I thought, *'I'm gonna do it! I'm gonna let him fuck me!'* It's kind of a weird feeling, ya know? Knowing I was gonna get fucked, wanting it, but never done it before, scared as hell, and didn't know what to expect, what I was supposed to do, but wanting it just the same. Behind me, I could hear Sanka taking off his clothes. I thought about the things I'd heard about black guys and their huge cocks. As bad as I wanted it at that point, I remember thinking, *'I hear anything other than his pants thump on the floor and I'm gettin' the fuck outta here!'*

Well, I didn't hear anything else thump on the floor so I relaxed. I turned over onto my back. Sanka was standing naked at the end of the bed holding his pants in his hand. I smiled at him. My own cock was solid as a rock and flat against my belly. The candles he had lit were those real thick ones, and they were very much used, so they didn't really put out a lot of light. The room was about as black as Sanka was, and, in my drunk and stoned condition, I couldn't see very well anyway. But Sanka turned to toss his pants over the dresser and I noticed a movement between his legs. I tried to focus my eyes and looked closer. At that time I didn't know what a Beer Can Cock was, but I'd just found out! His cock wasn't all that long but it was actually as thick as the beer can sitting right next to me. I realized he intended to stick that thing up my ass and it seemed the blood immediately drained from my cock and made a beeline to my eyes 'cause they were so bugged out.

Sanka took a look at me and started laughing. He normally had a cool laugh – sort of like Eddie Murphy's, but with a much higher pitch. This time though, I didn't even hear him laugh. I just stared at his cock. He was as stoned as I was and was laughing so hard now that he almost doubled over. I just stared at his cock. He reached into a bowl on the dresser and pulled out another joint. I just stared at his cock.

He turned around and sat on the bed right next to my head. Once his cock was out of view I was able to look at this face. He lit the joint and passed it to me. "Don' worry, mon," he said to me. He reached over and put his hand on my shoulder and squeezed gently. The laughter was gone now – he was serious. "This your first time, am I right?" I took a hit from the joint – a big hit – and only nodded. Some guys don't like popping cherries and I thought Sanka was one of them. So I relaxed again thinking I was off the hook.

"That's okay, mon, you'll do fine. Sanka will take good care of you."

There went my blood pressure again! Made my eyes bug out all over again as I realized that he *still* intended to split me right down the middle with that pole of his. Remember guys, I was stoned! *Way* stoned. Forgot I could say, "No." Besides, what little thinking I was doing at the time was about how I probably owed him. He wasn't charging me rent to stay at his place, so I assumed he was charging me sex. I wondered where he hid all the bodies after he got done fucking them.

Sanka took the joint from me, took a hit, and handed it back. I just held it like I didn't know what I was supposed to do with it. Sanka stretched out on the bed next to me. My body was as tense and stiff as my cock used to be. He took my hand with the joint in it and pushed it up to my lips and I finally took a hit.

"Hey, mon," Sanka said, softly. "Nuthin' we have to do yet. Don' worry, we take our time, okay? Besides, I promised you a massage first, and Sanka keeps his promises, okay?"

I let him turn me back onto my stomach. He had me keep the joint and started with my feet. I had to admit – he had magic fingers. He worked my feet one at a time, then started up my legs. By the time he worked his way up to my butt, I'd relaxed and was only thinking about how good his hands felt. He told me he would give me the best massage and he wasn't kidding. By the time he started kneading my shoulders I was moaning and feeling *real* good! The joint was finished and Sanka even kneaded my hands and my head.

He turned me over onto my back. I felt so good that my eyes were now closed and I didn't even open them when I turned over. Sanka was talking to me the whole time – real soothing kind of talk; soft, almost whispering. The sound of his voice came closer and closer; then, suddenly, I felt his lips against mine. I opened my mouth just a little and his tongue slid right in. I'd never kissed anyone before, at least not on the lips, but Sanka made me feel like I was a pro. I don't know how long that one kiss lasted, but it was my first, and I'll never, ever forget the feeling that sent shivers right down to my toes. Long before our lips separated my cock was hard again, and when our lips finally did part I realized that I had wrapped my arms around him and pulled him on top of me.

I felt the weight of his body on mine shift as he raised up a little. I don't remember if I opened my eyes, but I remember I opened my mouth. I don't remember if I said anything, but I remember that I wanted more, and Sanka obliged. I felt his lips brush mine again and I opened my mouth further. I felt the tip of his tongue touch the tip of mine. I slid my hands up his back to the back of his head and pulled him into me and devoured his tongue. I no longer cared how big his cock was. Now I was hungry. Now I was horny. Now I trusted him and now I wanted him. I wanted to get my cherry popped, and I wanted Sanka to do it.

My second kiss ever lasted as long as my first but was more intense, more electric because now I took part in it. When our lips parted once again I felt like I was ready. I spread my legs under Sanka and started to wrap them around him like I'd seen women do in the magazines hidden under my dad's bed. But Sanka raised up again. I started to say something, to tell him it was all right, to beg even, but his finger tips reached up to my lips and stopped me. My eyes were still closed. I was afraid opening them would somehow break the spell. "Sssssshhh," he whispered. "I'm not done yet, mon."

Then his hands went back to work on my body. From my shoulders to my chest. He rubbed my nipples and squeezed my pecs. I felt his mouth cover a nipple and he sucked real gentle. My head started lolling side to side and small moans escaped me. His tongue started working it's way down my chest with his hands just ahead of it. He was on his knees now and his hands slid down past my navel. I was sure he was going to grab my cock, but his hands separated at the last second and started kneading my thighs, and I felt a little disappointed. But I trusted him now, and I didn't say anything but just let him do his stuff. He massaged my legs, his hands sliding up and down each one, each time getting closer and closer to my cock, but always reversing direction at the last second. His lips kissed and licked – they too, getting closer and closer to my cock, but always skipping over it over and over again until I couldn't take it any more.

"Please!" I finally hissed. "Suck it Sanka!" I begged. "Suck it, man! Do *some*thing with it!" I was squirming on the bed, bucking my hips, trying to push my cock into his face, but he kept avoiding it. Finally, I raised my head and opened my eyes. "Damn it, Sanka!" I almost yelled. At that, I felt his hands slide in one smooth motion from my knees up my thighs. This time I knew he was gonna do it and I let my head fall back down. His hands slid up my thighs and one wrapped around my cock while the other cupped my balls.

"Ooohhhh!" the sound was more like wind coming from my mouth as my whole body arched up in the air. Sanka's mouth met my cock and swallowed it right down and I almost blew my load right then and there. I didn't know it at the time, but Sanka squeezed my cock hard and kept me from cumming. His mouth and tongue worked my cock just like his hands had worked my body. I thought I'd felt good before, but now I felt almost like I was having some kind of out-of-body experience, white light and all! Sanka stretched out on the bed 'til his own cock was right next to my face. I forgot all about how big it was. I only knew I wanted it any way I could get it. I reached over and wrapped my fist around it, and his cock and my mouth were like two magnets slamming together as I stuffed as much of it as I could into my mouth.

As much as I could turned out to be not much more than the head, but it sure did fill my mouth! I remember thinking, *'Hot Damn! I finally got a hard cock in my mouth!'* I sucked on it and licked it and slicked it up and jacked the rest. I let it fall out of my mouth and leaned over and sucked one of his balls into my mouth. I sucked it in and out and it bobbed between my lips and Sanka moaned. I don't know how much of Sanka's moans were me making him feel good, and how much was him trying to make me feel like I was doing good, but hearing him moan made me feel great! I stuck out my tongue and licked his dick all up and down and tasted his pre cum and sucked on the head, and Sanka drove me wild doing the same to me.

I don't know how long we 69'd it like that – I'd lost all track of time, and didn't care, either. Eventually, Sanka started twisting his body around 'til his cock fell out of my mouth. He worked himself around until he was stretched out between my legs with his feet on the floor, and my cock never left his mouth. I looked down my body and watched his head bob up and down, and saw my cock sink in and out of his mouth. Moans and grunts were coming out of my mouth all on their own. I wrapped my legs around him and this time he didn't tell me he wasn't done yet. He didn't tell me anything – he just kept right on sucking. His hand played with my balls and his tongue played with my dick. Then I felt both his hands on my thighs. They pushed gently and I soon saw my feet way up in the air.

Sanka's tongue went back to work. It licked my cock up and down the shaft and licked my balls. I felt more than saw, but one of his hands lifted my balls up and his tongue kept on going strong. Then I felt his hands back on my thighs, pushing. Pushing until my legs were spread as far as they would go and I felt like any further and Sanka would need to make a wish! Next thing I know, I felt Sanka's tongue enter the crack of my ass, and my eyes bugged out again. Sanka's tongue crossed over my hole and I crossed over into a whole other world.

There wasn't enough light to see my face, but my eyes squinted shut, my lips peeled back and bared my teeth, and I sucked in a huge gulp of air and let it out in one big loud, "Yesss!" I didn't know what I was doing at the time – Sanka told me later – but I started cheering him on. I was saying, "Eat me, Sanka! Lick my ass, baby! Eat the fuck out of me!" And this was coming from a guy who lived an extremely sheltered life, never saw a porn movie, never read a story, never kissed or made out before, and had no idea what was expected of me. The sensations were like shock waves starting at my virgin hole and exploding outward 'til they slammed into my feet and made my toes fan out and slammed my head into the pillow while grunts and yells shot out of my mouth.

Some things about fucking just come natural. When the pleasure kicks in, no one needs to be told what to do. I felt Sanka's hands grab one of my legs and pull, and I flipped over onto all fours without Sanka telling me to. My butt was in his face, which he rammed back in my crack; his tongue hitting a bull's eye in my hole. I reached a hand back all on my own. I didn't wonder if it was okay, or if I needed to let Sanka know what I wanted. I only knew I wanted more of his face in my ass and I grabbed the back of his head and pushed his face into my butt harder. I started wiggling my ass around and back and forth like I was trying to get his whole head in there, and Sanka moaned his approval. I stayed on all fours, but leaned forward and buried my face in the pillow. Over and over again I sucked in a breath of air and let it out in a grunt. Sucked it in and grunted. Sucked it in and yelled. Sucked it in and begged for more. I didn't think at the time, but it was a good thing we were in a house rather than an apartment. If there were people on the other side of the wall, I'm sure they would be jacking themselves off listening to the noise I was making.

I didn't see him do it, or know what he was doing at the time or why, but Sanka had reached over to his side somewhere and coated his finger with lube. I only felt his hot tongue replaced with something cold and wet. Then, suddenly, I felt something stiff slide up my ass with surprising ease. My head snapped around with my eyes bugged out yet again. I couldn't believe that the monster he had between his legs would fit that easily. I saw Sanka looking at me with a big smile on his face.

"Don' worry, mon," he grinned. "It's just my finger."

'Oh, crap!' I thought. *'There's more!'*

"Just relax, mon, and let my finger play a bit." I turned back around and buried my face in the pillow again. The apprehension was starting to come back as I realized what was coming next.

Sanka used his finger to work my ass for a while. I felt it slide in and out and he wiggled it around. He was sneaky all right, but still gentle as he slid two fingers up my butt. He wiggled them around and new waves of pleasure started bouncing around my body. Without realizing it at the time I started bucking my hips and riding Sanka's fingers. Where I couldn't get enough of his tongue earlier, now I couldn't get enough of his fingers. In and out they went. In all the way and wiggled around, all the time with me cheering him on and letting him know how much I liked it. Sanka told me how to push back against his fingers like I was constipated, and I felt my hole loosen up a little, and his fingers slid in more easily. He was telling me to do that when he was shoving his cock in, but I don't remember listening too closely. I only remember that I didn't want these new and wonderful feelings to stop.

I felt the bed shift as Sanka got up on his knees and positioned himself behind me. The mattress bounced and heaved but his fingers never left my ass. He told me he was going to pull his fingers out, then the next thing coming in would be his cock. While he still worked my ass with his fingers, he kept talking to me and telling me to stay relaxed, and promising me that he would only go as fast or as far as I let him. Then I felt his fingers leave my butt. I looked back and watched him move. I couldn't see what he was doing exactly, but he was lubing up his cock. He reached forward and I felt more of the cold stuff on my ass. He put the head of his cock up against my ass and I looked away, closed my eyes and gritted my teeth again. I sat completely still. Sanka used the head of his cock to spread the lube around. He told me once again to relax, and to push back against his cock like I was trying to push it away with my hole. Then I felt one of Sanka's hands on my back. He steadied his cock up against my hole. Then he pushed...

Now, I know a lot of you guys out there reading this haven't been fucked yet. The last thing I want to do is say something that would scare you out of taking that initial plunge because, believe me, getting fucked is the absolute most wonderful feeling there is or ever will be. It's better than being drunk. Better than being high on drugs. Better than anything I've ever felt before or since. The only thing that matches getting fucked by a hard cock is fucking a tight little butt with your own hard cock. I would want you guys to go for it, so I won't go into great detail describing the pain.

Suffice it to say I was on all fours when Sanka tried to shove his over developed fuck meat up my ass.

All fours left the bed at the same time. All fours hit the floor at the same time. All fours became a tangled mass of arms and legs and hands and feet and bugged out eyes as I tried to walk, crawl, stumble, roll, and run to the wall on the opposite side of the room, trying to get as far away from that man as I possibly could. If my hole had been an eye, and if looks really could kill, I'd be in prison today. But I promised not to go into great detail describing the pain (and I may have blown it already), so we'll leave it at that.

I wound up sitting on the floor with my back against the far wall and my knees up under my chin. Probably the only thing showing on my face was my bugged out eyes as I could only stare, speechless, at Sanka. Sanka was doubled over laughing that high pitched Eddie Murphy laugh of his. When he put a foot down on the floor, I was afraid that meant he was going to come after me again, and I immediately clasped my hands together in front of my hole...like that would help.

But he only put his foot on the floor to steady himself because he was laughing so hard. "Don' worry, mon! Don' worry!" he said in between snickers.

'Yeah,' I thought to myself, 'You said that before!' He turned around and stepped to the dresser. The pot I smoked was still in me full force, and as I watched his butt jiggle, I wished I could find a telephone pole or something to shove up *his* ass so he'd know how I felt!

He lit another joint, then turned around and leaned against the dresser. "It's okay, mon," he said. "We stop now for a while, okay? I promise." Then he doubled over again in laughter. I just kept staring at him, and

I hadn't moved yet. "Look, mon," Sanka said, still laughing. He put the joint in his mouth, grabbed a pair of shorts from somewhere, and put them on. "There, you see? I won't do nothing now."

Once I was sure he was serious about not coming after me again, I looked down between my legs, lifted my balls up, and gingerly touched my hole with the tips of my fingers. I thought it would be swollen or bleeding or something, but it wasn't. Sanka saw what I was doing and went into another fit of laughter.

One thing about pot – it makes you laugh. It makes you laugh a lot, and it makes you laugh at absolutely nothing. When I realized what I was thinking and what I was doing, I broke into a relieved kind of laughter myself.

"Here, mon," Sanka said and reached his arm out to hand me the joint. "Have a hit. It will make you feel better."

"No thanks!" I said, "You gave me some of that stuff before and look what happened!" Then we both laughed, him half on and half off the bed, and me up against the wall like I was in a rubber room.

Well guys, I did help Sanka finish the joint, and it did make me forget the feeling that I promised not to dwell on, and I actually did let Sanka try again. There was the thought in the back of my head that I didn't want Sanka to think I was a lousy lay, so I was somewhat determined to fit that Boa cock of his up my ass. The second time, he laid on his back and told me how to straddle him and sit on his cock. He said that was the best way to do it because I'm the one who remained in control of how much and how fast. I really tried, but I just couldn't fit that damn thing up my butt. I don't mind admitting it now because it was such a long time ago but I simply couldn't do it. We wound up lying on the bed drinking beer and smoking even more pot (Sanka seemed to have an endless supply), and talking about it.

Sanka told me I'm not the first or last guy to go through this, and I certainly wasn't the first guy who couldn't take his cock. Turns out he'd popped quite a few cherries before and not all of them were successful. He said he had a fuck buddy who had a cock about the same size as mine. Then he reminded me that he'd managed to get a few fingers up my butt and that I'd liked that, didn't I?

I smiled at him. "I sure did!" I said, and leaned over and kissed him. He was right. I most certainly *did* enjoy him finger fucking me. I thought he was going to offer to get me off with his fingers. Instead he offered to call his buddy to come over and fuck me. I got nervous all over again, but we'd smoked more pot and drank more beer, and I figured (as well as I was capable of "figuring") that it was gonna have to happen sometime sooner or later, so I might as well get it fucking over with while I was at least with someone I trusted. So I told him to go ahead.

—

Sanka went into the living room to call Mike, his fuck buddy. I sat on the bed with my legs crossed and wondered what else I'd gotten myself into. Sanka came back in the bedroom with yet another joint in his mouth. I learned later that he kept those things *all* over the house. Whenever he or I was in the mood to light one up, we didn't have to go far to get one. He was carrying two more beers and handed one to me. He was still wearing the shorts and stretched out on the bed on his stomach, and we smoked and drank and laughed and talked about a lot of things. In our drunken and stoned state we solved many of the world's problems, found a cure for cancer, and determined that in one of our previous lives we saw God. Then the talk came around to sex.

"Have you ever fucked a girl, mon?" Sanka asked me. This wasn't a locker room – in high school or anywhere – so I told him the truth. No, I haven't. He asked me if I ever did anything at all with a guy and I told him about a couple times of mutual jackoffs, and one quick suck with a guy from a neighboring high school.

"So," Sanka said. "You never fucked a guy either, right mon?" I just shook my head. "Well," Sanka smiled. He looked up at me with a strange, conniving look on his face and grinned. He reached back and patted his own ass. "So! What's wrong with right now, eh mon?"

Before I could speak, Sanka scooted up on the bed, pulled me down and kissed me. We made out for a while and he played with my cock, which responded immediately. I started to think that I still owed Sanka.

He'd taken such good care of me, and didn't get pissed when I couldn't take his dick up my ass. I thought that I should try somehow to get him off, and the idea of finally getting to stick my dick up another guy's ass seemed the perfect way to do it. And a lot of fun, too!

I scooted out from under him and rolled on top of him. I pulled his shorts down his legs and off: threw them behind me somewhere. I started rubbing his legs and butt like he did to me. Sanka just put his arms under his face and laid there, moaned encouragement and wiggled his ass.

He had a muscular ass. Two globes that I squeezed and rubbed and pulled apart and pushed together. I ran my fingers up and down the crack and felt his hole while he moaned and closed his eyes. He wasn't telling me to do anything, but just lay there and let me do what I wanted. I played with his butt, and leaned over and kissed each cheek, licked his thighs like he did to me. My own cock seemed to get harder and harder and I couldn't wait to feel it in his ass. I leaned up on my hands and knees and lowered my cock into his crack and started dry humping his butt while I moaned some myself. It felt wonderful being on top of him with my cock almost in his butt; so good in fact, that I still enjoy dry humping a guy's ass even today.

Sanka had heavy curtains over the only window in the bedroom, so I didn't notice that the sun was starting to come up. The candles by his door were burning dimmer, so I couldn't really see what I was doing as Sanka was black enough to simply blend into the darkness of the room. But I didn't need to see – I only needed to feel. And I was feeling good. Sanka laid still and moaned while I slowly slid my cock up and down the crack of his ass. He flexed his butt cheeks and I felt them tighten up against my cock, and I could have shot a load then, but I knew what I wanted, and I wanted to fuck him.

I felt the head of my dick slide across his hole so the next time I held it there and moved my hips in a circular motion. Sanka thought I was going to try to shove it in and reached back to stop me.

"No no, mon," he mumbled. "Use the lube first."

"Oh yeah!" I said and gulped. "Okay." And then I thought to myself, *'What's lube?'* I scratched my head. Sanka was lying with his eyes still closed and a big smile on his face. I thought he was feeling really good, because I remembered that I sure did when he was working on me. I didn't want to ruin the moment for him, so I didn't ask him anything. I felt the shelf next to the bed, and found two jars and a tube. One jar was open so I took out a tiny bit of the stuff inside and sniffed it. It was Vaseline, but it didn't feel like the stuff he used on me. I wiped it off and squeezed a bit from the tube. *'Yeah!'* I thought, *'This is it! This is what he used on me! Hot Damn!'* So I squeezed some more on my fingers and spread it all up and down Sanka's ass with one hand, and all over my cock with the other.

"Mmmmmm yeah!" Sanka moaned.

'Yeah!' I thought. *'He likes it! I'm doin' good!'*

"Oh mon, thassss good!"

'Yeah, I'm gettin' him goin'! All by myself!'

"Good, mon, good!"

'Oh yeah, baby! I'm hot! I'm hot!'

"You picked de right one, mon."

'Oh SHUT UP!'

Sanka laughed and got himself up on all fours. I finally realized that I wasn't fooling him and stopped trying. I positioned myself behind him and put the head of my dick up against his ass. My hands were really slippery from all the lube, and it felt good to be slowly jerking myself and poking Sanka's ass, and…and…well…I couldn't find his hole!

I pushed my cock but it just slid up the crack of his ass, or it slid down and tickled his balls. I tried several times, but I'd used an awful lot of lube, and it was dark, and Sanka was black, and I couldn't *see*, okay? Sanka was still laughing and I was getting pissed with myself. I couldn't stand the thought of failing yet again, and my cock started to go a little soft, and that scared me even more. I leaned back and jerked myself, closed my eyes and thought of how good it felt when Sanka ate my ass, and worked my cock hard again. I moved back into position behind Sanka. He very smoothly reached back, grabbed my cock and put it up against his hole and held it there. He told me to push, and when I did he pushed back, and I entered heaven!

It didn't occur to me at the time that Sanka was a lot more experienced than I was, so when my cock slid all the way up his ass to my bush, my eyes bugged out again because I was afraid he would hurt like I did. But Sanka just started rocking back and forth, sliding his ass up and down my cock. I realized he was just fine, that he wasn't hurting at all.

I said before that some things about fucking just come natural. My hips acted like they had a mind of their own and I just started bucking them back and forth, driving my cock in and out of Sanka's ass. I grabbed hold of his hips, leaned my head back and moaned. Sanka stopped rocking back and forth and now the only movement was me fucking my first ass!

'Oh shit!' I thought, *'I'm doin' it! I'm doin' it! I'm FUCKING!! YEAH!!'*

I tightened my grip on Sanka's hips and started fucking faster. I looked down and watched my own dick appear and disappear in and out of Sanka's ass. I couldn't believe how good it felt. I went faster, started driving my cock in his butt harder. I kept glancing at his face, looking for a sign that I was going too fast or too hard. All I saw on his face was a big smile, so I fucked him faster and harder. Soon the mattress was bouncing and we were both moaning and I was grunting with each thrust. I no longer worried about hurting him or whether or not I was doing it right or where I was or what day or year it was. Twice I pulled back too far and my dick fell out of his ass. But I was too hot to worry about it. I just grabbed my dick and shoved it right back up his ass and kept right on fucking. I listened to my hips slapping his cheeks and felt my balls slapping his balls and I started yelling out each time I slammed my cock up that butt.

Far too soon for me I knew I was going to shoot and I couldn't hold back. Didn't know how to anyway. I yelled that I was gonna cum, and Sanka just said to do it. So I jack hammered his ass and shot my load and screamed and just kept right on fucking my dry dick up his butt until I broke my concentration and it fell out of his ass by itself. I let out one more long moan and collapsed on the bed next to him. I looked up at him and he leaned over and kissed me again. I broke away from his lips and panted and tried to catch my breath. After a couple of minutes I was calmed down some and Sanka leaned over to my ear.

"You did great, mon. Best fuck I had in a long time! Thanks, mon." Then he kissed me again.

I really can't describe how good I felt. Not only did I finally get to do some fucking, but it was all I thought it would be and more. I think that no one has done an adequate job of putting the feelings into words, and I'm only going to ask you guys to take my word for it. Well...mine, and millions of other guys'! And to top it off he *thanked* me! He actually told me I did a good job!

Sanka rolled over and lit yet another joint, and then we heard a knock on the door. I'd completely forgotten that Mike was coming over, but I felt so good about what I'd just done that I was even able to ignore the nerves that tried to steal their way back into my feelings. Sanka went into the living room to open the door and I heard him greet Mike and tell him we were in the bedroom. The sun was up, but the room was still in darkness except right at the doorway where the two candles were, and a little sunlight that filtered in from the living room. I lay in the bed still recovering and thinking of how good I felt, and the next thing I knew, Jesus Christ walked into the room!

—

Well...not really, of course. But in those days there was no real dress code. No real fashion statement that when seen today would make someone immediately think of that time. The flashy bell-bottoms and disco style of dress hadn't happened yet. Hairstyles were still having men (including me) with hair parted in the middle and at least shoulder length, as mine was. The only headgear wasn't hats, but headbands. Other than that, it was pretty much anything goes.

I don't mean to be blasphemous, but religious pictures showed Jesus Christ as a blonde. He had shoulder length hair that just happened to be parted in the middle. In many pictures, Jesus also had a mustache and beard. Parents were trying hard to get us kids to cut our hair, and our answer was usually that Jesus had long hair and so can we.

Well, guess what Mike looked like? You got it – he was a blonde. And his hair was parted in the middle, *and* it was shoulder length. Mike took things a step further, and in the style of Toga parties, fashioned a sheet into an outfit that looked like what was worn in biblical times, right down to the sandaled feet, and he even grew a mustache and a short beard. The complete ensemble earned himself the nickname, "JC." So after a whole bunch of beer and a generous helping of pot, you can imagine my first thought when Mike walked into the dimly lit doorway! Made me swallow hard and gulp.

After that first instant, Mike greeted me, shook my hand, and I finally realized that he was just a mortal like me, and I wasn't about to be punished for anything I'd done so far. The three of us sat and drank and smoked and talked for a while. Then Mike came and sat on the bed next to me.

Sanka and I were still naked, and Mike put his arm around me and asked me if I was okay with everything so far. I was a little apprehensive still, and was trying to think of a smooth way to ask him to take off that ridiculous outfit! In what I considered a gutsy move, I decided to show him that it was okay, and wrapped my arms around him and kissed him. He returned the favor, and we wound up laying on the bed making out in the semi darkness. We were laying side to side and my hands were sliding all over Mike's body while his hands slid over mine.

My hands did have something of an ulterior motive. I was really floating in the clouds from Mike's lips and tongue, but I still felt rather silly thinking I was laying naked in bed making out with a biblical figure. Especially that *particular* biblical figure! My hands and fingers slid over his chest looking to unbutton his shirt so I could get it off. But since what he was wearing wasn't really a shirt – there were no buttons. And since he wasn't really wearing pants, and it wasn't really a dress, there was no snap or zipper or anything I expected.

"Hey, Mike?"

"Yeah."

"Could you do me a favor?"

"That's what I came for," he said sensually. I rolled my eyes.

"I mean something else."

"Sure, babe," he said. No one had called me "babe" before, and it felt good. And like dry humping a guy's ass it stuck with me, and is my favorite term of endearment today.

I grabbed a handful of whatever it was Mike was wearing. "Would you please get rid of this?" I asked him, then snickered. "I feel like I should pray or something." That was silly, but it made us both laugh. I noticed when we were laughing that I didn't hear Sanka's high-pitched laugh. He had left the room and left Mike and me alone. Mike reached behind him where I couldn't see, and made some kind of movement. He stood up and everything came off all at once and he stood naked in front of me. Now he was beautiful! His cock really was the same size as mine, and it stood up straight and proud. Since he now looked normal, my own cock woke up.

Mike pushed me back on the bed and laid on top of me. He kissed me again and my arms automatically wrapped around his back. This time when my hands explored his body, they were rewarded with a smooth back and a nicely formed butt. Mike's tongue was as magic as Sanka's and I was soon lost in the moment. My own body started slowly squirming, my cock searching for Mike's as he laid on top of me. Mike reached between us and pulled our cocks together, then pushed his hips and applied pressure that made me moan. I kissed him and let him kiss me, and my hands got to know his back, my fingers combed his hair, played with his ass, rubbed his hole, and our lips stayed together.

Mike reached between us again and grabbed my cock. He squeezed gently; just enough so that when he raised his body up a little, the pressure on my cock remained constant. His lips finally let mine go and moved to my ear, "I'm gonna make ya feel good now, Robby," he said. I only moaned my approval. I couldn't think of anything to say, "Just relax, babe," he told me. "I'll make it slow and easy and wonderful." All I could do was nod. His lips kissed my ear, my cheek, my neck, and moved to my chest. I ran my fingers through his hair and he licked my nipples and lightly raked his teeth across them. I didn't know until then how sensitive my nipples were, and I reveled in the sensations. Mike's tongue worked one and his fingers worked the other; then they traded places while his other hand stayed around my cock. When his tongue wasn't sliding across me, his beard was, and it was just rough enough to send new shivers rippling across my body from one end to the other and back again, and all I could do was moan while my head lolled from side to side and I just laid there, panting and smiling.

Mike's lips worked their way on down my body, and soon his hand around my cock was replaced with his mouth, and his tongue worked it's magic again. I kept wondering what I'd done to deserve to experience so much pleasure all at once. One hand moved down between my legs and played with my balls, and Mike sucked and sucked and I still could only moan. I reached down and grabbed his head, but didn't know what to do with it and could only keep running my fingers through his hair. His tongue ran up and down my cock and licked my balls and sucked them one by one while his hand slid further down.

His fingers slid into the crack of my ass and across my hole, but the apprehension I expected to start feeling didn't come. He didn't have to push anything; my legs spread by themselves. I don't know where it came from or when he got it, but I felt the lube as he spread it over my hole and his fingers rubbed and prodded. My hands reached down and I spread my cheeks myself and Mike's fingers accepted the invitation. They rubbed some more and prodded with a little more pressure and while his mouth worked my cock his finger slid into my hole and I didn't even flinch. I only moaned some more.

Mike was patient. It felt like he was taking forever working my hole with his finger and my cock with his mouth. I can't remember noticing when, but there was a moment when I realized he had two fingers up my ass, and I just took a deep breath and let it all out in a hiss. Mike kept making magic on my cock and ass, and the next thing I knew, he let go of my cock just long enough to tell me that he had three fingers up my ass and that I was doing great. He managed to spread my hole further and further with his fingers and my butt didn't complain at all. I didn't even notice him shifting position and didn't open my eyes to see that he was up on his knees with his mouth still on my cock and his fingers still up my ass.

I didn't even have time to tell myself that this was it, or that the time had come. I only felt Mike's lips leave my cock, which slapped against my belly. His fingers kept sliding in and out of my ass, and in and out, and then they slid all the way back out. When they slid back in I realized it wasn't his fingers – but his cock! There was no pain, no sting, nothing but the same sensations: only more intense because now I finally had a hard cock up my ass for the first time, and I went nuts! He slid his cock in and out of my ass at the same speed his fingers had been moving and kept up the same rhythm and I felt great! When I realized what he'd done, I opened my eyes and could only stare at him with wide eyes and an equally wide smile. He was looking right into my eyes and smiling. I couldn't think of anything to say to match what I was feeling, so I only stared at him while he picked up the pace. Finally he threw his head back and started moaning himself. His long hair was swinging back and forth while his mouth formed an "O" and he panted and grunted and so did I.

I thought I wasn't doing anything special for him, but I didn't realize what a virgin ass felt like – what the psychological effect of popping a cherry was. Mike was having a good time and I was amazed at how easy I took his cock up my ass, and how fucking great it felt. Like a lot of virgins, I couldn't hold back and didn't need to hold or jack my cock. Cum started shooting out all on it's own and splatted on my chest and belly. My moans changed to pants and whimpers and my hands just fanned out while my arms raised up in the air as I shot my load all over myself. My legs had found their way over Mike's shoulders and he had to grab my ankles to keep them from squeezing his neck too tight.

Watching me cum sent Mike over the edge. He bared his teeth and started pounding my ass and I didn't care a bit. He slammed my ass hard enough to make my hair shake and then he rammed his cock all the way in and held it there and just ground his hips. I felt a strange sensation of his cock throbbing in my ass, and realized he was filling my ass up with the first load of cum I ever had, and it was indescribably wonderful! He pulled his cock out of my ass and sat back on his knees. I reached down and felt his cum oozing out of my hole. I sat up and saw a few drops of cum still working their way out of his cock. Anyone watching would have thought I was in some kind of trance. I just looked at Mike's cock, then up at Mike, then back to his cock. Mike reached out and pulled me into a hug and told me I was wonderful and beautiful, and I wrapped my arms around him and kissed him.

A thought occurred to me, and in what I'm sure was a typically virgin'ish fashion I cupped Mike's face in both hands, and looked right into his eyes only an inch away from his face. "I got *fucked!*" I yelled, and Mike laughed. I let go of his face and pumped both arms in the air and yelled, "Yesssssss!" and wrapped Mike back into a bear hug. Mike laughed some more, and this time I heard Sanka's high pitched laugh as he appeared at the door, still naked.

Sanka came and sat on the bed and the three of us hugged and kissed. Sanka shook a finger at me. "I *knew* you would do it, mon!" he told me. "I knew you would do jus' fine!" and we hugged again and kissed and acted silly for a while. I finally thought to ask Sanka where he'd been, and while I was floating on Cloud 9, and while the earth moved and the angels sang and all that, Sanka was in the kitchen ignoring us and calmly fixing a meal. I then noticed the smell of breakfast and realized that the pot had done the other thing it's famous for, and I was ravenously hungry. The three of us sat naked at the kitchen table and in typical cone head fashion consumed mass quantities of bacon, eggs, hash browns and toast. Between bites, poor Sanka and Mike had to listen to me babbling on and on about what felt good and what felt best and what felt better and how good I felt 'cause I was a *man* now. After we ate, somehow the three of us fit on the bed and slept the rest of the day away. When we woke up I started talking again, and I'd bet you that if you asked the two of them today, they would say that when I went to work that evening they were glad to get rid of me.

I stayed with Sanka a couple of months, then got my own place. I kept seeing Sanka and Mike along with a couple of other fuck buddies of theirs for the next two years until I was 20. Even though I was having a great time with them, I was still desperate to get out into the world and *do* something with myself.

Almost on the spur of the moment, I joined the military. I didn't tell anyone right away because – thanks to Vietnam – being in the military was not a cool thing to do. I didn't care though, because I just wanted to leave and go somewhere else and do something else and be someone else. I ran into Sanka on the street four days before I was due to leave for boot camp and told him where I was going. This time it was *his* eyes that bugged out like mine had done that first night.

"What you go and do a crazy thing like that for, mon?" he gasped and even felt my forehead to see if I had a fever. When he realized that it was all arranged and done, the contract was signed, and I had already raised my hand, he insisted on having a going away party for me. He told me there was one other guy I needed to meet.

"I didn't tell you before, mon," he said. "It was no accident I came to Papa C's that night." I just looked at him, puzzled. "There was another guy you know who told me you were in a jam," Sanka explained. I thought of the couple of guys I jacked off with in high school and the guy from the high school in the next town who's cock I sucked. I wondered which of them it was. I'd seen them on the streets, but we never did do anything else with each other, and I thought that one of them had gotten a job in another city and had moved away. I'd gotten an apartment in the town next to my hometown and, hadn't been back home in two years. I smiled, wondering how I could ever thank whoever it was for starting me on a road I was only too happy to keep traveling, but Sanka wouldn't tell me which one it was. He wanted to surprise me, which was something about him I'd gotten used to.

The party was a rip roaring one involving Mike and the other guys, and we drank and smoked and danced, and later turned the whole thing into one big orgy. I really don't remember how many times I got fucked, or how many butts I sank my own cock into. Then there was a knock on the door. I was in the bedroom and Sanka came in and told me my buddy was here. I almost ran from the bedroom to see which of my old school playmates it was. I almost broke into tears as I ran across the room to give him a hug...

It was Papa C.

∎

THE CLUB

Most guys tell stories about how they helped other guys over their shyness. Thought I'd tell you one about other guys having to help me; even though I was hot, horny, and couldn't wait. Sounds weird, huh?

In spite of my shyness, I'd already lost my virginity. Loved it, but couldn't wait to get out of the dumpy, backwards, tiny little town I lived in. I didn't have any money and was too scared to just get up and leave. The only sure way I could think of to leave; and yet have somewhere to go with a nice job waiting for me, was to join the military. See how desperate I was?

Well, guys, it worked! I got outta that town all right. Wound up living with 79 other guys in a one bedroom house. No living room. No kitchen. One really huge bathroom. It's called boot camp.

I know you're already thinking about what I had to do to keep from popping a boner in the showers, but you know what? After a long day of marching, physical conditioning, getting yelled at, more marching, an obstacle course, still getting yelled at, maybe a class or two, then more

149

marching, I was way too exhausted to think about anything other than hitting the sack and getting some sleep. And that happened every day!

But that's not what I want to tell you about.

After boot camp came technical training: what we simply called tech school. Lots of cute guys there but still no luck. So me and my blue balls couldn't wait to get to my first assignment where I could get my own place and get fucked as much as I wanted. The first thing I learned was that I was going overseas – but didn't know exactly where. I thought it would be great since at the time, I thought Europe was more open and accepting of gays.

One still has to be careful, though, being in the military and all. Even though it would be Europe, I would still have to live and work according to the military's rules. The only important part about Clinton's "Don't Ask – Don't Tell" policy is the "Don't Tell" part, but that was relatively easy. The hard part was waiting until I could actually get to Europe and start cock hunting.

Well…they didn't send me to Europe. They sent me to Asia. To a dumpy, backwards, tiny little base that reminded me a lot of my home town. Just different people. *Shit!*

There were about 500 active duty stationed there; some with families who lived off base. The single guys like me lived in the barracks. Another house with one really huge bathroom! But I did get the chance to move off base and live with a straight guy in an apartment he already had. He was looking for a break in rent and expenses. I worked days – he worked nights. *'Perfect'* I thought. So I moved off base.

The first and last thing everybody did entering or leaving the base was to pass the Security Police shack at the Main (and only) Gate. Since the base was small, everybody knew everybody else, and everybody saw everybody else, but the most visible people were, of course, the Security Police. And *man* were there some cute guys on that force! There were three or four I'd picked out, and jacked off in my apartment thinking about what I'd do to them if I had the chance.

It had been about a year since my last fuck, and in spite of how horny I was, I was still too nervous to approach anyone myself. Those guys made my dick perk up every time I saw them walking around the base in their tailored uniforms with those utility belts framing their crotches. Jeez, I was horny all the time!

One night, I had been at the club on base and was leaving about 2:00 in the morning. I walked to the gate. There were buses that ran downtown, but only until 11:00. Some taxis would park outside the gate, but, as the night wore on, there were fewer and fewer. When I reached the gate there were none. The Security guy on duty at the gate was one of the cutest SP's on the base. I waved to him as I passed, crossed the street, and sat down on a bench to wait for a taxi.

Toby, the Security guy, stuck his head out of his shack and said something to me about the non-possibility of getting a taxi at that hour. People get lonely out at that gate, so I went back to the shack, leaned against the door, and me and Toby shot the shit for a while. I said something concerning the absence of women on the base. You know, gotta talk the talk.

Toby said something I can't remember, but then he looked me square in my eye and said, "But I don't need women – ya know?" My knees got weak. My mouth dried. I wanted to jump on him right then and there. Of course, I would never do that. Besides, it still could have been a military trick to identify gays in the military.

So I said, "No, whadda ya mean?"

Toby took one step that brought him so close to me, I could feel his hot breath in my ear. He said, "I mean this," and reached out and grabbed my crotch and started kneading my dick through my jeans. If I weren't already leaning against the door of the shack I would have fallen over backwards!

Toby pulled me to his face and kissed me. Deep, hard, and wet! He shoved his tongue toward the back of my mouth as far as it would go. I couldn't believe my luck so much it almost made me dizzy. I reached behind his head and held his lips to mine with one hand and went for his crotch with the other. Sure enough, his dick was rock hard in his pants! Toby then pulled me inside the shack, kicked the door closed, unzipped my jeans, reached in, and grabbed my cock through my underwear – all without letting go of my lips.

I remembered where we were, pulled away and said, "Man, we can't do this here!"

"Sure we can," he said. "Just watch the windows and let me know if you see car lights coming. There's plenty of time. Don't worry, I've done this before." (He *has?*)

Toby went down on his knees, pulled my pants down, then my underwear. My cock popped up, slapped against my belly, and Toby caught it in his mouth and he swallowed it whole. I thought I was gonna go right through the roof! After a year of only fucking my hand, and finally I'm gettin' sucked, gonna suck, *and* with one of the guys I had been fantasizing about to boot!

Toby stood up, said, "My turn!" and dropped his pants. Like him, I went down on my knees, pulled his underwear down, and caught his cock in my mouth. Heaven! I thought I was in heaven. His dick wasn't overly large, but a bit longer than average, and just fine with me. I sucked his dick, played with his balls, rubbed his ass, and fingered his hot tight hole for I don't know how long.

Finally he pulled his dick out of my mouth and told me to lean over the stool in front of a small table they used as a desk. I eagerly dove over the stool and spread my legs. "Come on, man!" I said, "Come *on*! Hurry up before somebody comes up here!"

I felt something cold and wet on my asshole. I thought, *'This dude carries lube to work with him!...Cool.'* Toby used the head of his dick to spread the lube around my ass. Used it to tickle me, tease me, made me beg for it. Then he shoved his hard cock into my ass; all the way, in one shove.

It hurt, but my moaning had nothing to do with pain. Toby fucked me right there in the guard shack for all he was worth. Just slammed his cock into my ass over and over again. In and out, in and out, he went.

All the way in, then stopping to grind his hips, moving his dick back and forth. Then more slamming. I had to reach my hands out and grab hold of the table to keep from banging my head against it. I didn't need to jack my dick to help me cum. I just started squirting all over the stool. Bit my lip so I wouldn't scream out. I felt Toby's cock throb as he shot his hot cum into my ass.

"Yeah!" I said, softly, more to myself than to Toby. "Fill me up, man. I wanna ooze your cum for days! Do it, man, shoot that load *all* the way up in me!"

Toby finished cumming, pulled his dick out of my ass, pulled his underwear and pants up, zipped up, adjusted his buckle and utility belt... and I was still spread- eagled over the stool, thanking my lucky stars.

"Get up," he said. "My relief will be here in a few minutes."

I was like a bullet coming off that stool. Got real clumsy about pulling my own pants back up. Even fell against the side of the shack a couple of times. Must have looked quite a sight, had anyone been watching.

"How soon?" I asked.

"Actually, he's a couple minutes late." Toby said.

"*Shit!*" I said. "Next time you think we can cut this a little bit closer?" I wanted to run back to the taxi bench, but then Toby's relief showed up. It was just after 3:00 AM. We had been sucking and fucking for almost an hour.

Toby told Shawn, his relief, that he was going to walk me back to the barracks, like I was just entering the base instead of leaving it. I humbly followed him down the deserted street, him walking confidently, and me tripping over every rock.

"Good thing no cars came through," I told him.

He looked over at me and grinned. "Whadda ya mean?" he asked. "Three of 'em came through when you were on your knees sucking my dick!" He just laughed while I 'bout shit.

But that's not what I wanted to tell you about, either.

Something occurred to me on the way to Toby's room. "What about your roommate?" I asked.

"No problem," Toby said. "He's on leave. Won't be back 'til Monday." Then he grinned that shit eatin' grin of his and said, "Besides, if he was here, he'd join us."

Good thing it was dark. I think my eyes were still bugging out when we got to Toby's room. I must have looked like a 14 year old virgin to anyone who may have been watching. There was the extra bed in Toby's room but I didn't use it. I don't have to tell you what happened after we entered. It'd make this lively tome too long. I slept with my finally soft dick tucked into the crack of Toby's ass. Woke him up the next afternoon when it got hard.

Now this is what I wanted to tell you about.

Toby told me to stay the weekend in his room with him. He didn't ask me. Just told me. Said a few friends were coming over later that evening. I just looked at him.

"Yeah," he grinned (*again!*). "We're gonna have some fun." We talked, we went out to eat, we talked some more, but Toby was being strangely quiet about what was up for the evening. I was feeling a little apprehensive from not being able to get any more information from him, but then I did kind of already know everyone. Wasn't exactly like I was going to meet complete strangers. And besides, as small as that base was, if anything wacko was going on here I would have heard about it through the grapevine, right?

Little did I know.

By 9:00 that night there were seven other guys in that room. They came in one at a time and I was introduced. I was beginning to get annoyed. Everyone was quiet. I mean, no one said a word to lead me to believe anything other than an evening of beer and talk was going to happen. I kept looking to Toby for some kind of sign. I silently swore that some day I was going to fuck that grin of his right off his face!

At nine the 7th guy arrived and announced to no one in particular, "I'm it. Everybody else is at work. Jimmy's in the hall." He came over to me and shook my hand, "Hi, Robby," he said. "Been waitin' for ya." (*Huh?*) At that, shoes and socks started coming off all over the room as everyone started undressing. I just sat there like the village idiot. Toby sat down next to me and finally told me what was going on.

These guys were, of course, all gay. They had been getting together like this for quite some time. Not all of them were SP's, but all were known to me – if only by sight. I had talked to a couple of them quite often, and was a little shocked to see them there.

It was kind of like a club, I guess. Certainly nothing that was written down – not in the military! There was really only one rule – silence. About the most secret kind of club there could possibly be. Membership was by invitation only, and tonight was going to be my "initiation."

Toby said I could refuse, and at any time during the night I could say to stop. I would then be expected to leave, and none of the other guys would ever mention it to me again, and I would be expected to keep quiet about it myself. But I also wouldn't "Belong", and none of the other guys would have me again either. Finally, I was able to give Toby a shit eatin' grin of my own. "Let's go," I said. Then I thought to ask, "Who's Jimmy – in the hall?"

"He's the lookout." Toby said. "On his word, we all start gettin' dressed. It means somebody's coming." I just nodded. Seven naked guys came over to me and started pulling my clothes off, and Toby kept talking to me.

I was expected to take them all. One at a time. Starting with the smallest cock up to the biggest. One down my throat, one up my ass. Until they'd all had me. They moved a bed into the middle of the room, piled with pillows. I was laid across the bed, my feet on the floor, my ass in the air, and my face just over the other side. They called what was about to happen an "initiation." I called it Heaven on Earth. An outsider would have called it a gang bang.

I didn't really care what the fuck it was called; I just wanted to get *on* with it! Toby was first. Slid his dick in my mouth and I clamped down on it. Someone else started working my asshole with cold lube. I started sucking Toby's dick. I reached over to grab hold of it, but Toby pushed my arms back down.

"Reach down," he told me. "Grab your dick. Don't cum!" He held my head still and slowly started fucking my face. I didn't even have to move. I really didn't have to work at all. I wasn't expected to show them a good time. I was only expected to take what they were giving me. And *that* I was more than happy to do!

After a while, Toby pulled his now slippery cock out of my mouth and a dry one took it's place. Toby moved down to my ass, slapped some more lube on my hole, and slowly slid his cock in. Didn't really hurt. A slight sting was all but I didn't care. After a few minutes of being full of 2 hard cocks I had to really squeeze my own cock tight to keep from cumming.

Well guys, that's how it went. One dick would pull out -another would take it's place. These guys knew what they were doing. No one was particularly rough. No real butt slamming. Just kind of slow but steady fucking – both my ass and my face. I kept my eyes closed. Not from worry – from ecstasy. Just as I would think someone was about to cum he would pull out. But before my ass could close completely another dick would slide in.

Sometimes I wouldn't even notice it was a different dick, but other times it would stretch my hole a little further or it would slide in a little deeper. A little more sting, but always with fresh cold lube.

How long did this go on? How the hell should I know? Time was the last thing I was thinking about! My head was way too far up in the clouds. Even lost count of how many dicks went in and how many were left. These guys were cool. Also very, very quiet. None of the usual grunting and groaning. No words, either. No ooohhhhhs, or aaahhhss, or yyyeeeaahhhs. In a way it was weird, but like I said, I didn't care. I'd never had anything even close to this happen to me before and I was reveling in it!

Eventually a dick pulled out of my mouth but no other took it's place. It was actually difficult to close my mouth. Then the last guy pulled out of my ass. Someone said, "Turn over," and I felt several hands help me flip over onto my back. Tried to open my eyes but the lights were too bright. Was about to smile when I felt something hot and wet splat onto my chest. Then another on my leg. That's why none of them came inside me! They were saving it for now.

Next thing, I was ready to swear it was fucking raining cum! They had circled me and were jacking themselves off – and creaming me like I'd never been creamed before or since. I reached down to my own dick and added my own load. Felt like a cake that had just been frosted. I even felt a splat or two on my feet.

Toby then lay right on top of me and kissed me again. Very gentle and long kiss. He raised up and said, "You did great." There was even a smattering of subdued applause. I still had my eyes closed, but I sensed Toby's shit eatin' grin. I just reached up, grabbed his head and pulled him back down on me, smearing the cum all over him. Kissed him deep and hard. I didn't care that there were other guys in the room. I turned Toby's head until his ear was against my mouth. "Thank You!" I whispered.

Toby slid off me, then more hands helped me sit up. I wiped cum off my eyes and opened them. The other guys actually came up and shook my hand. One handed me a towel. Toby took a towel and wrapped it around himself; took mine and wrapped it around me. The last guy who had come in stuck his head out the door and said something to the guy who was in the hall. He nodded, looked at Toby and me and said, "It's clear."

Toby took me down the hall to the shower. I was literally in a daze. I walked out the door of his room and just stopped. Looked around without really seeing anything. Toby actually had to grab my hand and *lead* me to the shower. We walked down the hall, all covered in cum. I even heard a couple of drops hit the floor. I stayed in the shower at least 15 minutes just standing there letting the water run over me. Every few minutes, I would shake my head, mutter something like, "Damn!", "Wow!" or "Fuckin A!" I didn't have to look at Toby, I knew he was grinning.

After the shower, I had come back to earth and was able to walk back to Toby's room by myself. I said earlier my head was in the clouds. I hadn't even thought that we were in a military barracks, and anyone could have come into the hallway while me and cum covered Toby were walking to the shower. I didn't even notice that some of the other guys were walking in front of and behind us just to hide us.

When we got back to Toby's room, everyone had left except Shawn, the guy who relieved Toby the night before. They told me another startling revelation. The first was that Shawn actually showed up *on time* to relieve Toby last night, and had stood in the dark watching Toby fuck me. Toby had seen him coming and had waved him off. He also gave Shawn a thumbs up, meaning I had passed the initial test. Apparently, I was able to take a slam bang fucking according to their first rule – silently.

After all, it wouldn't do to have anyone walk down the hall of the barracks and hear the sounds of fucking coming from one of the rooms without the sounds of a female mixed in. So, in our group, silence was definitely golden! Shawn told me he was a "Short Timer," meaning he was transferring out in three weeks. I was now officially the new kid in the club.

"How long has this been going on?" I asked them. Shawn told me that when he was "initiated" there was another guy who was a short timer who told Shawn that when *he* was initiated there was yet another short timer who told *him*... etc, etc, etc. No one knew how far back it went. Seems I had just become a member of a very large club. I then asked them, "But how did you know? I mean, how did you know I'm gay?"

They had a whole set up; refined over the years. Soon after I arrived at that base, I was watched. Everybody was. Eventually a gay man will do something, say something, move a certain way, hold their cigarette a certain way. Every gay man does something to send out the gaydar. Whatever it was I did, one of the guys picked up on it. That guy told the others, as was expected. Then they all started watching me.

I was at that base a full 6 months before that night. I was watched, evaluated, discussed, and eventually, approved. Remember I said I had talked to a couple of the guys often? It was all part of the screening process. It was determined by all of them that I would be "acceptable," meaning that I would keep my mouth shut.

Then the guy would be approached; (get this), usually by an SP, usually at the gate, and usually in the middle of the night! In other words; it was a set up from day one. But, as you know, I didn't care.

Obviously, my life at that base changed. I moved back into the barracks and this time I was happy. I became a "watcher" along with everyone else. And I took part in four other initiations while I was there; including one I had recruited myself, meaning it was my job to lure the guy to the barracks, let everyone else know, arrange a night when most of them could be there, and see the guy through it as Toby had done for me.

By the time I transferred out, I was the short timer telling the new kid in the club this weird kind of legacy he was expected to continue. All of the other guys who initiated me had transferred and left. I was fucking around with a completely different group of guys then. Toby transferred a couple months before I did. We quickly lost touch and I don't know where he is today.

I guess you guys have noticed that nowhere in this epic piece of literature have I named the base – or even the branch of service – and I never will. Although I've been gone for years, I'm sure it's still going on. I'm sure I could go back there, go back to the same barracks, and every now and then I'll see some guy sitting out in the hallway reading something, but facing the door, looking out.

If I said where this place is now, probably nothing would happen. But it would make it a little easier for me to tell someone else, thinking nothing would happen, and again, probably nothing will. Eventually though, I would open my mouth once too often, and terrible things would happen to whoever is there now. It's difficult enough for gays in the military to hook up as it is. Leave those guys alone. Let 'em have fun.

And Toby, wherever you are – grinning – Thank You!

■

ABOUT THE AUTHOR

David Solomon has been writing for the past several years. This is his first published collection of short stories. David writes on various subjects, injects some personal opinions and thought provoking ideas in his stories, but always leaves his readers with smiles on their faces. He lives and works in Milwaukee, Wisconsin.